# Thundersloth!

# Thundersloth!

## Stephen Kappotis

Cape Ann Press
North Andover, Massachusetts

The Second Voyage of Sloth and Good Boy
Cape Ann Press
North Andover, MA, USA

Copyright © 2025 Stephen Kappotis
First edition 2025
Edited by Tony Amato
All art work by the author

Paperback: ISBN 979-8-9859352-3-3
Ebook: ISBN 979-8-9859352-5-7

Library of Congress Control Number: 2025907786
10 9 8 7 6 5 4 3 2 1

For the non-human animals and the people of compassion.

# Back in the Saddle

Livestock animals, car exhaust, food cooking, and drying laundry—Good Boy the German shepherd's nose tells him that he's finally home even before he emerges from the tree line and the bug-filled shade under the tall canopy of trees. It had been a long few days navigating the rainforest and now he makes his way down the road to pick up his friend, Juan Manuel, from the farm where he stays with other landscaping goats while Good Boy is away with Shriya on digs. Shriya is the paleontologist Good Boy lives with. And now, she has been captured.

A donkey brays loudly from around the bend and, as soon as Good Boy turns onto the dirt drive alongside the fenced field where the goats are, Juan Manuel spots him and runs over, beating Mace, the protective herd donkey to the fence. Juan Manuel, a large, brown Spanish goat, stares down the donkey for a moment, then the donkey recognizes Good Boy and, with a snort, heads back to the bulk of the herd, keeping an eye on Good Boy just the same.

Juan Manuel turns to Good Boy.

"She's never going to like me." Good Boy growls.

"Donkeys don't like dogs. Your kind can't be trusted, you know!" Juan Manuel jokes.

Good Boy snorts. "With what some of them did to Calypso's mother, you won't get an argument from me."

"Where's Shriya?" Juan Manuel asks.

"We were with these male people in the jungle and were attacked by big monkeys and a smelly bear that knocked me into a ditch. When I got back to the path, everyone was gone."

"Taken or eaten?" Juan Manuel asks, taking a step back.

"Taken. I followed their smell down the path, but there were too many monkeys for me to handle alone."

Juan Manuel looks surprised. "How big were these monkeys?"

"About the size of people."

"How many were there?"

1

Good Boy looks down at his paws and tries to think, then looks across the field of goats, "About as many as there are hooves in the field—*more*."

Juan Manuel looks across the field. "Think we should take some of them with us, then?"

"I don't think we can fit them in the boat."

"Boat? How far is it?"

"Far. The skyfire rose and fell about my feet worth of times walking. It will be much faster by boat."

"Then where's Calypso?" Calypso is a brown Bradypus sloth who was rescued as a baby after her mother was killed shielding her from attacking stray dogs and raised with Good Boy by a man named Pablo Rios. She now lives in the forest not far away and she knows how to drive the boat, which has special controls.

"I was going to get her next."

"Yeah, great idea!" Juan Manuel nods sarcastically. "These monkeys sound like formidable enemies, so let's grab our small friend who can be outrun by a turtle!"

"She really dislikes monkeys, though."

"Yes, she does. Is it true that they fling their poop?"

"If Calypso says so, they probably do," Good Boy sniffs. "I didn't see much of the big ones, and I've only seen little ones up close when they got drunk on old fruit and fell out of the trees."

Juan Manuel paws at the ground and looks up, thinking. "The three of us against a lot of big monkeys and a smelly bear. Why not?"

"I'm sure the people will fight, too."

"If they're still alive," Juan Manuel frowns.

"If they aren't, then we'll try to leave without being seen, but don't think like that."

Juan Manuel nods. "You're right. We took on a whole restaurant of people by ourselves, so how bad can some monkeys be?"

Good Boy lowers himself to the ground and pulls a thorn out of one paw with his teeth. "You didn't see these monkeys."

"Do they have guns?"

"No . . . I don't think so."

"Those people had guns."

"Do you know how to get out of here?" Good Boy asks.

"There's a gate up there, but . . ." Juan Manuel backs up and with a few quick hops, climbs and leaps over the fence into the driveway. ". . . this is faster than messing with the latch." A couple of goats in the field bleat encouragement and he takes a quick bow.

A slim, tanned man of slightly shorter height in tan pants and a short sleeve shirt yells and waves from the door of a house behind the goat barn up the driveway. "Buca! Charleston!" he calls. Hearing the shortened version of Bucephalus, the name Pablo, had given him, Good Boy feels a flash of urgency to rescue Shriya.

"We should bring Miguel," Juan Manuel says, acknowledging the goatherder.

Good Boy rises back onto his feet. "We don't have time to try to get him to understand what we need to do or how to get there."

"You remember?"

"Yeah, I'll smell where we need to turn the boat in when we get to it, then it's just up some flowing small water until we see the other boat."

Miguel comes running down the road toward them.

"OK, time to get Calypso!"

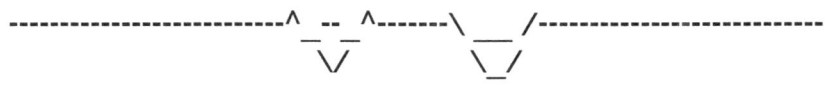

The patter of his predator paws on the pathway disturbs the conversations of the smaller animals and insects of the rainforest on either side before Good Boy's nose recognizes that they're in the right place as they arrive under a tall cumaru tree. He looks into the foliage far above and barks to announce his presence. A gray Bradypus sloth with a male sloth's dark yellow and black striped patch on his back in the next tree over looks down at the disturbance with irritation until his nose recognizes the dog and the goat. He stops munching leaves to call down with a shrill squeal and get their attention.

Good Boy looks up.

"Wrong tree!" the sloth says in the common language shared between domestic animals and some wild animals, like the sloth, who live near them and care to learn.

"Swimming sloth! Is that you?"

"All sloths swim, you know."

"You never gave us a name!"

"Calypso did," Juan Manuel says to Good Boy.

"Yeah, but he doesn't like it."

"Hi, Juan Manuel!" the sloth raises an arm with his claws folded in as a greeting instead of the warning they'd convey if they were fanned out.

"Hey, Drunk Monkey!" he yells back up.

The sloth blinks slowly. "I don't like that name."

"Aw, come on, that's funny!"

"Monkeys are terrible."

Good Boy gives Juan Manuel an impatient glare.

Juan Manuel nods to the sloth, "I hear they throw their own poop."

"I don't know, but they're very noisy and they run all through the branches and do not respect someone wanting to be left alone."

"Do you know where Calypso is?" Good Boy asks.

The sloth hangs from his back legs and scratches his chin for a long moment.

"We're kind of in a hurry, here!"

"Everyone is always in a hurry."

Good Boy waits for a more useful reply, but isn't getting one.

Another few moments go by while the sloth dislodges some moths from his fur.

"OK, so, do you know where she is?" Good Boy turns in a circle a few times and barks with impatience.

The sloth stares for a moment and points into the woods, "I think she's about . . ." he taps the claws of his hands together, ". . .my top hands and a bottom hand of claws of trees that way."

"Thank you!" Juan Manuel says.

Good Boy looks at Juan Manuel, "What does that mean?"

"Well, sloths have the same number of claws on each hand as I have hooves . . . or do they have one less?" He looks up and squints, but he can't tell from the ground. He frowns at Good Boy. "I don't remember. Can't you smell Calypso out?"

"Sloths just smell like earth and mosses and that kind of thing. Even the dirty ones smell like algae. They'd make great hunters and be able to sneak up on anything if they weren't so slow."

Juan Manuel sighs. "It can't be that far. After we find her, maybe we should go back and get Miguel in case we end up needing him." They begin walking in the direction indicated by the friendly sloth.

"We won't need him and we still have no way of telling him where to go. You know the people can't communicate silently like we can."

"Calypso will drive."

"Do you think he'll just leave her to do that?"

Juan Manuel gives a raspberry with his lips. "That's true, but is it really that you don't want him along because you don't like him?"

"Me not liking him has nothing to do with our inability to communicate what we need him for. Also, he doesn't like me, either."

"He's pretty good to us goats, so maybe he doesn't like dogs."

"Maybe he's part donkey."

"With so many of these big monkeys that captured Shriya and the other people, it sounds like it would be much better if we had a person along," Juan Manuel says. "You don't like him because you're jealous that Shriya spends time with him without you, but that's also why he'll be useful."

"That's not at all why I don't like him."

"Oh, it definitely is."

"Shut up, goat, what do you know about —"

Some kind of fruit hits the ground not far from Good Boy's head and splatters. He looks up to see a brown Bradypus sloth waving at him.

"Good Boy!" Calypso calls down.

"We need your help!" Good Boys shouts back to her. "I know you're doing your thing here, but Shriya has been captured."

"Where's the goat person? Wouldn't he be better help?" Calypso asks.

"We need someone who can drive the boat."

She nods. "He's a person! He can drive the boat!"

"How do we explain to him where we need him to go?"

She scratches her head for a moment. "How's the boat?"

"It's been fixed! That's why we need you! The place where they took Shriya is too far through the rainforest to walk the whole way."

"The boat only works in the water," Calypso says, starting along her branch toward the tree trunk.

"Funny. We need to take it along the big land and up a flowing small water. Then we'll have to walk."

"Not me, I'll ride." Calypso pauses her hanging crawl along the branch. "How did you get back here without a boat?"

"I had to make my way through the jungle. Took many sky fires, so we need to hurry."

"Everyone always needs to hurry," she frowns. "So, who captured her?"

"Some kind of horrible giant monkeys!"

"*Monkeys?*" Calypso nods, transferring to the tree trunk. "I was getting bored, anyway." Some twigs full of leaves flutter to the ground. "Can one of you grab those bundles of leaves for me so I have something to eat on the boat?"

Juan Manuel gathers the bundles in his mouth and would complain about the taste, but doesn't want to drop them. Then something bites his lip and he lets them go. "Something bit me!"

Good Boy looks over the leaves to see some ants fleeing onto the soil. "It was those little things. They live on these kinds of trees. I tried to climb one once playing with Calypso, but I didn't try twice."

"Don't they bite her?"

"No. Everything likes Calypso," Good Boy says.

"Except for jaguars."

"No, they like her, but for a different reason."

Juan Manuel looks all around at the trees and vines. "Should we grab lunch while we wait for her?"

Finally seated on Good Boy's back, Calypso locks her claws around his collar and Juan Manuel again picks up the twigs with his mouth, ants thankfully gone on their way back to the tree.

"Hang on tight!" Good Boy announces.

It's been a while since she's felt the rush of a fast ride on his back, the blur of the rainforest on each side of the road, hanging on as tight as she can with her claws around his collar and her bottom hands—*feet*—gripping his fur, the weakness in her muscles as she tries to hold herself up to keep her stomach from bouncing off his back. Juan Manuel easily keeps up alongside.

They reach Shriya's neighborhood by skirting the river at the back of several other properties until they get to a short wall. They hop down into the small yard made up of a patchwork of various grasses and weeds between the back of Shriya's house and the river. The 5.5 meter speedboat is tied to the dock. The bullet holes from their previous voyage have been patched up and the boat repainted green, with a long, undulating sea serpent in place of the old stripes along the sides of the hull, but Calypso can't see color and doesn't notice the serpent. What she does notice is that the sliding fighter plane style canopy is open, pushed back over the tapering rear section of the cabin area.

The friends rush down the dock and see that the boat is loaded to go with a rifle, backpack, people food, water, and spare fuel tanks. Calypso works to untie the bow line while Juan Manuel drops the leaves inside the boat and gets the line at the stern. Once those two are free, they all climb inside and Calypso lets slip the final, central line that she reaches from the bench seat in the front just as Miguel comes running from the house, shouting and waving a book.

Calypso sits behind the control stick and hits the start button, but nothing happens. They start to float away from the dock. Suddenly, she remembers the lever under the dash and reaches for it, but Good Boy is faster and he flips the stick that extends the battery switch for her with his paw.

"I always forget that," she says, lowering the outboard motor by pulling back on the control stick and hitting the start button. It whirs and grumbles awake. Reaching for the throttle with her left hand, Calypso thinks about all the other times they'd escaped dangers by boat and is glad to not have anyone shooting at them this time.

A loud splash, and something flies inside the boat and bangs into the hull, rocking the boat side to side before it leans toward the dock. Miguel's arms reach into the cockpit and his head appears over the side. He starts to pull himself in and Good Boy barks threateningly at him.

Calypso wraps her claws around the throttle handle.

"No, help him in!" Juan Manuel says.

"Why?" asks Good Boy.

"Because seeing one person chopped up from the spinning fins that make the boat go is enough for me, and Miguel isn't trying to kill us!" Juan Manuel grabs hold of one of Miguel's sleeves and Good Boy grabs the other one. They mostly manage to tear his shirt, but he's able to drag himself inside. He sits down in the open floor behind the seat, takes the boonie hat from where it had been blown off to hang down his back from a string around his neck, and puts it on his head before taking off his pants and wringing them out.

"Now we're stuck with him!' Good Boy grumbles.

"Yeah, but he brought a gun, so I say he's better to have along than not."

"There's spinning fins that make the boat go?" Calypso interrupts.

"Yes, you can see them spray the water backwards when we move. How did you think it worked?"

She spots her special sunglasses hanging from the throttle lever and slips them over her head so she can see something beyond the boat besides the glare from reflected sunlight. "I didn't think about it. I just drive them, I don't know what makes them go." She turns her head almost completely backwards to see that everyone is sitting down behind her and then reverses into the river.

# The Smell of Thunder

Miguel looks around at Buca and Charleston sitting next to him on the open floor behind the front bench seat. In torn and soaking clothes he rubs his bruising arms and watches the sloth sitting on the cushion like a tiny person and wearing some kind of weird sunglasses made up of straps to hold them on her head. He cannot believe she is maneuvering the boat through the waves, but she is.

He figures Shriya must have made those glasses, though he can't imagine why. He shakes his head, thinking about how brilliant and odd she is and wonders what's weirder—that Shriya made sunglasses for a sloth and taught her how to drive the boat, which she can actually do—or that these animals conspired to steal the boat from him.

And were they going to find Shriya? Obviously, if Buca is back without her with his fur looking like he'd been walking through the jungle for a few days, something must have happened and he has come back here to get his friends for help. Shaking his head, Miguel picks up Shriya's field notes and scans through them for clues as to where she might be, trying to distract himself from thinking that she might not be alive. For now, he trusts that they somehow know where to go.

The notes imply that Shriya might have gone up a river to meet, Rondo Julius, an archaeologist friend from university who had contacted her about looking at a large paleotoca he had found, ancient cave-like burrows believed to be made by extinct megafauna, possibly one or several species of giant ground sloth. One so far north into Central America would make it a unique find and, naturally, being a paleontologist who specializes in extinct megafauna, Shriya was interested in seeing it.
Miguel looks up again at the sloth driving the boat and wonders how smart the large ones might have been before getting back to reading. Rondo Julius and two local scouts were looking for a previously unknown ancient city that he had discovered when going through some older LiDAR survey shots of the jungle that

had been overlooked when a research project lost its funding years earlier. The laser reflections of the LiDAR were able to see through foliage, water, and topsoil to create a 3D map revealing features that would be difficult or impossible to spot from the ground. Without the power of the LiDAR, an ancient monument or building covered in centuries of soil and vegetation might seem like nothing more than a natural hill, even when walking on top of it.

Shriya noted Rondo's excitement about finding this city that for centuries had avoided the eyes of scholars and hands of greedy looters. Previous stories of the lost city had been based entirely on accounts from indigenous people, passed down through generations, so many scientists doubted its existence, especially where it was rumored to have resided so far south from the accepted borders of the ancient Mayan civilization. Perhaps it wasn't Mayan, but now there was solid evidence that its ruins exist.

At some point, Rondo and his scouts followed a recently trampled and regrown path to a cave system that looked like it had been dug out by the claws of the enormous animal some of the indigenous people called a mapinguari, a jungle beast in native folklore similar to a smellier, bigger, and meaner North American Sasquatch. Immediately recognizing it as a paleotoca, and knowing Shriya wasn't too far away, Rondo contacted her from the closest village to see if she might want to take a look, and then waited there for her to get back to him.

Miguel stops reading to wonder what kind of friend of hers this Rondo is, and whether he should be jealous, or afraid for her safety. He looks at Buca and wishes he could ask him what he knows about this guy, then frowns, and flips a few pages looking for more information about where she might be. All he's able to find is a map with a small river and its coordinates, along with the location of the village where Rondo and his guides were waiting. Miguel flips through the last few pages, but there's not a single suspicious word about Rondo. Absorbed in his thoughts, he jumps in surprise as Charleston lays his head on his shoulder.

"Bahahahaha," the goat says.

Miguel scratches Charleston's head and guards the edges of the book in case he's thinking about eating it. Juan Manuel gives him a raspberry and turns to Good Boy, "He thinks I'm going to eat his book! Please, any goat knows they taste terrible!"

"But they're fun to shake and tear apart!" Good Boy says.

"I don't think he'd like that, either. How far do we have to go?"

"Pretty far."

"Oh, good," Juan Manuel says. "I was getting worried that I wasn't going to have enough time to be bored."

Overhearing the complaints, Calypso pushes the throttle farther forward and adjusts the motor trim. Miguel is watching her, so she gives him a slow blink, then turns back ahead with her characteristically unhurried manner.

Miguel decides to sit on the bench next to her and Good Boy stands up in back, placing his head between them. Miguel angles the book toward him and points at the map, but it means nothing to Good Boy. Calypso looks over at it and Miguel points to the land along their left. Calypso doesn't understand, so she looks at him. He points again at the map, tapping his finger on the spot where he thinks they are, then pointing back out at the land. Calypso slows the boat and sticks her head closer to the map to get a better look. Miguel traces his finger from where they are to the river they need to travel up and Calypso taps the river on the map.

"You got it! That's where we need to go!" he laughs, nodding. "How can you be this smart?"

Juan Manuel sticks his head over Good Boy's shoulder to see what's going on, but it doesn't look any more interesting than before. Calypso pulls the throttle back to neutral and climbs over the bench seat and onto Good Boy as the slowing boat starts to roll dramatically with the waves. Miguel just looks at her stupidly, so she taps him on the shoulder. He slides over to take control of the boat and the two big friends lie on the cooler floor in the back with Calypso staying warm on top of them. The boat smooths out as Miguel accelerates it up the coast toward the river.

"Why are you letting him drive?" Juan Manuel asks Calypso.

"He knows more than me."

"Good Boy knows how to get there."

"But the man has something that tells him where to go," Calypso insists.

"How does he know where to go if he wasn't there with her?"

"It's on the thing he's looking at," Calypso says.

Good Boy nods. "The people use books to tell each other things without having to be near each other. Pablo used to scratch in one when we went out to get the guns from the big water."

"What?" Juan Manuel asks.

"The guns! He would get them from under the water."

"Are you trying to tell me fish make guns?"

"I don't know *what* makes them. Maybe those dolphins? They're smart."

"They don't have hands!"

"Maybe there are people that live underwater," Calypso says.

Good Boy cocks his head a bit while processing that thought. "Yes, I think they do, because Pablo would put something in the water and then a box would float to the surface with guns in it, and then he would take the guns and sink the box again, then scratch in his book."

Calypso blinks slowly. "What was it that gave him the box of guns?"

"I don't know, I only saw the box come up."

"OK, so they scratch stuff in books, but how do they know what another person's scratches mean?" Juan Manuel asks.

"I have no idea."

"I think it's some kind of language," Calypso offers. "You know how they can only talk to each other with noise? Maybe they have this other silent way of talking, like we do, but with scratch marks. It's like the boat has those small twigs that point to scratch marks on the faces. The twigs turn more the faster the boat goes, so I think those scratch marks say something, but I don't know what they mean." She scratches herself and thinks for a moment. "Maybe it says when the motor needs the smelly juice."

"Smart," Juan Manuel says. "Still, I never saw Miguel drive a boat, so I'd be less nervous if you were driving."

Calypso yawns and picks up the stem of leaves Juan Manuel had carried for her to eat. "The people know how to do that kind of thing and I get tired from driving."

"How do you get tired when you're just sitting there?"

"I'm not just sitting there. I'm looking as hard as I can at everything, turning to meet the waves so the boat doesn't shake, adjusting the go handle, holding myself up." She taps her head. "It tires my head."

"That seems weird, but I can't drive, so I couldn't know." Juan Manuel turns to Good Boy, "How much longer, do you think it is until we get there?"

Good Boy lifts his head up, looking out at the land, then lowering it back to the floor. "I don't know why I looked. I'll know when we get to the river. The only part I remember about the big water was that it took a long time."

Eventually, Miguel stops the boat and steps into the back to grab one of the extra fuel containers, which he carefully pours into the main fuel tank filler on the gunwale, occasionally looking to make sure they aren't drifting too close to shore.

Calypso watches him carefully and concludes that she isn't strong enough to feed the boat its smelly juice, and her friends don't have arms, so it's a good thing this person is along. Miguel finishes, puts the half-empty container back, and restarts the engine.

14

Good Boy's nose picks up familiar smells and he looks up to see that they're at the river and barks in excitement. Miguel turns to him.

"Do you know where to go?" He slaps the seat for Good Boy to come up front and Good Boy sits down next to him. Miguel navigates the boat into the river and they travel up through the mangroves.

After a little while, the smell of cooking fish excites Good Boy, the mangroves clear away at the banks, and they pass by an open space with a few small homes made of rough-cut wood with corrugated metal panel walls and roofs of either reeds or corrugated metal. A few people are standing around a fire. They stop and look curiously at the fancy boat. Miguel waves to them and a few of them wave back. Once past the people, they enter a darker, overgrown area where the trees and vines reach out over the water, blocking and filtering much of the sunlight. Birds squawk and take flight from both sides, and monkeys jabber at them. One monkey follows them from branch to branch for a short distance before losing interest. Calypso climbs over the back of the seat and onto Good Boy to take advantage of the view in the eye-friendly low light. She sniffs the air—rain is coming. A big dragonfly lands on her arm, its wings droop with stuttered movements as it munches a fly it has caught. When it's done, it sits for a moment to rest, then flies back out of the boat.

What there is of light goes dark suddenly, so Miguel closes the canopy and turns the vent on full power as the heavy rain rolls over the area. With the turn of a switch, wipers sweep across to clear the windshield. Reaching under the middle of the dashboard, he pulls a lever that rotates a circular door in the deck at the very front of the bow that brings up an infrared camera. A screen flips out of the top of the dashboard to display a clear black and white image of the sides of the river and the overhanging rainforest. When he turns his wrist on the grip of the control stick, the camera turns and the view on the screen follows as he sweeps it side to side. Bright white blurs hide or duck into the foliage as the boat approaches them. Amazed,

Calypso climbs next to him and leans toward the strange window to get a better look.

"Are you trying to learn?" he asks her. She looks up at him and he takes her clawed hand and puts it under his as he continues back and forth sweep.

Just then, an awful smell permeates the cabin, causing Miguel to shake his head in complaint. Calypso sticks her nose into the vent and takes a breath of cleaner air to fill her lungs and hold her breath.

Juan Manuel sticks out his tongue. "Blech, I can tell what you ate!"

"That doesn't smell anything like what I ate," says Good Boy.

"I can tell by the taste!"

"Oh, like you never fart!"

"I don't fart when we're all stuck in a closed space."

"What am I supposed to do? Dummy is the one who closed the boat up."

"Because it's raining!"

"Well, it's not healthy to keep them in!"

"It's not healthy for the rest of us when you don't!"

"I heard from another dog that his friend's brother's butt exploded when he held a fart in too long."

"I don't believe that any dog has ever done that!"

"His person was getting mad at him for it, so he was trying to keep her happy."

Through watering eyes, Miguel notices Calypso with her nose in the vent for fresh air and laughs. "Smart!" he tells her. "Who was that, huh? It wasn't you, was it?"

She lifts her head and slowly turns to give him what he would notice as an insulted look if he was able to recognize it.

"Must be the dog, huh?"

"Who else in here eats rotting dead squirrels?" Juan Manuel asks. Miguel hears only a bleat of desperation.

"Hey, that's exactly what I ate!" Good Boy says, impressed.

"Told you I could taste it," Juan Manuel nods.

"Do you see that?" Miguel points to a large blur on the screen ducking down against the riverbank ahead. "That big white spot might be a jaguar."

Calypso freezes and Good Boy gives off a low, guttural growl.

"It's OK, it can't get in here. The funny thing is, it could be a black jaguar or a spotted one, but it would look the same on the screen because the camera shows the body heat, not the color."

Calypso looks through the window, but doesn't see the jaguar. Other than understanding that there's a jaguar outside, she doesn't know what Miguel is saying, but she sees that the boat has a special eye and how to move it to see through the leaves and rain. She turns to Good Boy, "Did you know about this?"

"Yes. Pablo would use it when I went with him at night."

"He never took me with him at night."

"It was more dangerous." Good Boy squints his eyes at the memory as if looking far away.

"Obviously, with the jaguars."

"No, because of the other people he'd meet with."

"Like the ones that killed him?"

"Yes. The feeling I'd get from those people . . ." Good Boy shakes his head.

Miguel watches in awe as the animals appear to him to have a silent conversation that ends with Buca shaking his head and the sloth looking back at him. "I know you can't possibly understand what an infrared camera is, but you get how to move it, don't you?" He lets go of the grip and puts her hand back on it. She turns her wrist and the camera swivels back and forth, but she loses interest as tiredness overcomes her and she yawns.

"You're such a smart little sloth!" Miguel says. "Shriya told me she rescued a sick sloth, but I thought she brought you to a sloth sanctuary, and I figured they must have released it back into the wild by now. I don't know why she taught you to drive . . . or how . . . then again, you probably learned quickly."

He looks at Good Boy. "Were you all going to try to find Shriya on your own?"

"Of course, dummy!" Good Boy barks.

Miguel shakes his head. "I really wish I could talk to all of you."

Good Boy closes his mouth in a frown. "Who'd have thought that in a group with a goat, a sloth, a dog, and a person, it would be the person who is the dumbest?"

"Obviously," Calypso says, "nobody would have thought it was the sloth."

"Oh, so what are you saying?" Juan Manuel asks, exchanging looks with Good Boy.

Lifting herself with her claws on the back of the seat to look in back, she smiles, "I don't know, but I think the next smartest animal on the boat wouldn't have to ask."

"I would agree with that," Good Boy nods.

Juan Manuel makes a fart noise at them with his lips and sits back down.

"I don't think this person is dumb," Calypso says, thoughtfully, "he's just smart in different ways, like we all are," she says.

Around nightfall, Good Boy's nose registers a long-awaited smell, so he barks an alert just before the camera picks up an inflatable boat that looks like Shriya's, pulled up onto the embankment. The inside of the Speedwell is horribly stuffy under the closed canopy, but the cloud of bugs swirling around the slow-moving boat shows it to be preferable to leaving it open, even with the smell of Miguel's bug repellant burning the noses of the friends worse than the petrol. The substantial top of a massive fallen tree reaches into the river, de-limbed from someone cutting off its branches, which should work as a makeshift dock to tie up on. Miguel shuts off the camera and pulls up to the tree, sliding the canopy open just enough to hook a line to the remaining stub of a cut branch and to the retractable cleat on the side of the boat to hold them while they wait for the bugs to disperse a little.

Miguel confirms that the boat is Shriya's by the name *Great Auk* on the transom, but Good Boy knew by the smell and has already told Calypso and Juan Manuel . With the Speedwell secured to the tree properly, Miguel sets up a tent on the remains of a camp that is just big enough for everyone and he lets them stay inside, except for Calypso, who opts to climb one of the trees next to them and eat and sleep up there. Miguel wonders if she'll come back down, but isn't too concerned, as she won't be much help. Though he thinks the likelihood is remote, to make sure she doesn't take the boat, he reminds himself to disconnect the ignition before they break camp.

The next morning, Miguel catches some fish and cooks them on a fire for himself and Good Boy to eat, while looking through the book.

Juan Manuel munches some brush and watches Calypso crawl over to them from the bottom of the tree. "I didn't know sloths danced."

"I wasn't dancing."

"Yes, you were, I could see you dancing behind the tree."

"She was pooping," Good Boy says.

"Oh," he nods. "I understand. I once ate something that stuffed me up and I was so happy to finally be able to go that I felt like celebrating. Come to think of it, I've never seen you go before."

"Sloths only go about," she holds up her clawed hands one after the other, "this many claws of rising sky fires apart."

"What? So, three mornings, then another three mornings?" Juan Manuel looks at Good Boy. "How many is that?"

"It's . . . three, then there's . . . It's more than five," Good Boy says. "Too many."

Juan Manuel turns back to Calypso. "Yeah, no wonder you were celebrating." He munches some more leaves as she continues crawling to Miguel. "You even look thinner!" He makes a fart noise at her and she ignores the comment.

19

Miguel closes the book. "Hey, you decided to join us again! Do you want to come up here?"

She reaches out and he picks her up. She looks at the book and doesn't understand what he's looking at, but he points to it as if he thinks she might, which she appreciates. He takes out a loose sheet of paper and unfolds it.

"Do you see this?" he asks quietly. "This is a three-dimensional image from a survey plane of an ancient city. It's a mystery who built it, because it says here that this is too far south for a Mayan city."

She blinks at him, liking how his quiet voice sounds to her.

He moves his hand in the air. "An airplane flies over the rainforest and takes these images using lasers that see through the vegetation. This ancient city has been hidden in the jungle for centuries. Do you know how many generations of sloths that is? Must be a couple hundred."

He looks down at the sloth who appears to be listening intently, though Calypso is actually comprehending almost nothing.

"How high of a number can you even conceive? They say bees can count to four or so, but why would a sloth need to recognize a number much higher than that? Five maybe?" He smiles and scratches her head and she closes her eyes.

Juan Manuel comes over to look at the pictures, but doesn't see what's so special about them and goes back to eating.

Good Boy watches Miguel pull out a small object and stare at it. He then points at the photo and presses some buttons on the device. Miguel puts down the device and says to Good Boy, "The latitude and longitude of the city are written on the images. Between my GPS and your nose we should be able to follow their path to the city. I bet it's about a six-hour hike."

Several hours beyond six hours later, Calypso is riding on Juan Manuel so Good Boy can be free to better sniff around the trail and everyone's hot except Calypso, who's more comfortable with the heat and hasn't had to trudge through the jungle for a large part of the day.

Miguel follows at the back, hacking at the foliage with a machete when necessary, but the path had been cut through by Shriya and Rondo and his guides, so it hasn't fully grown back yet.

"How did you get back from here without a boat?" Calypso asks Good Boy.

"I followed the path back to the river."

"How did you get across the river?"

"I swam much of the way until I was near where the people live. Some of them gave me food. Then I made my way down some more paths to the . . ." he sniffs the air and the ground along both sides of the trail then continues, ". . .coast and swam across. I picked up more trails along the water that led me back. I even went by that place with the cows. The bad place where the people eat haven't taken another sloth, unless they were keeping it in the front. I checked when I grabbed another plate of food someone left too close to the railing."

"That's good. Did they chase you?"

"No, it was different people."

"What about crocodiles?"

"Didn't see any." Good Boy stops again and looks down another path that cuts through the thick forest.

Calypso and Juan Manuel follow his gaze. "Yeah, what is that?" Juan Manuel asks.

Good Boy's nose twitches. "Don't know."

"Jaguar?" Calypso asks nervously.

"No, it's something different."

"Bad different, or just different?" she asks again.

"Bad, maybe? They *smell* bad."

"What do you mean, *they*?"

"More than one," Good Boy answers, not really paying attention to anything but the smell.

"Yes, I know what *they* means. How many?"

21

"There are several big monkeys and . . . something else." He aims his nose in a circle, then back in the direction they're heading.

The friends keep walking, but slower, and more cautiously. Miguel hasn't noticed anything yet.

Suddenly, the path widens, with clearance tall enough for a truck, though no truck could navigate so well around the large trees and rough terrain.

"There's a split," Miguel says, looking down the new available route—a space like a tunnel framed by knocked-down small trees, broken branches, and new shoots of recovering vegetation on bare soil. He decides to head down the short distance to where it ends in a clearing about the size of a football pitch in front of a flat cliff covered in roots and vines.

A large cave entrance in the cliff face, surrounded by scattered soil and stone dug out from the hole, lines up almost directly with the path, and a feeling of foreboding comes over Miguel as he steps toward it. This must be the paleotoca, but the dirt from the cave looks like it has only been there a short time, not thousands of years. Tentatively sticking his head inside the entrance, it just smells like a cave. He's a bit surprised to not see any bats hanging from the ceiling, but figures they must be farther inside.

Good Boy barks behind Miguel, and if the roof of the cave were any lower, he'd have smashed his head on it in surprise. He takes another look around the clearing and motions for Buca and the goat to head back to the main path. Good Boy obeys and Juan Manuel follows him.

They stop back at the trail and watch Miguel examine a bit of brown fur on a broken branch. He pinches the long, thin hairs between his fingers but they aren't familiar. He notices Good Boy's gaze.

"What is it, huh? Could it be a bear?" Miguel looks all around them. "This far north ... or south?"

Good Boy barks an affirmative warning.

"Did he say, *bear*?" Calypso asks.

"Yeah, like we saw on Pablo's magic window. I thought that's what it might have been, but all I saw was a giant paw and claws like bananas."

"Those big animals that eat the jumping fish you told me about a long time ago?" Juan Manuel asks.

"Yeah," Good Boy answers.

"Do they . . . eat anything else?"

"Goats," Good Boy says.

"Not funny."

Miguel walks back past the friends a short distance in the original direction before turning back to Good Boy. "Which way did they go?"

Good Boy looks at his friends. "Keep an eye behind you. You'll definitely smell the bear, but the smell is so strong that you won't know how far away it is, and the giant monkeys will hide in that smell cloud. If Miguel disappears or gets attacked, scream and we'll all run."

"Every one of us except for Miguel," Juan Manuel snorts.

"And me," Calypso says. "I'll be hanging on to you like a tree branch in a big wind!"

Good Boy walks past Miguel to lead them on the original path and everyone follows. Miguel notices Calypso has her head turned around to look at him and he wonders why.

After a bend in the path, they come to a clearing around a stream where they stop to take a break and drink. Miguel crouches down and pours water through a filter in a bottle, waits for it to drip through, drinks a large amount of it, then refills the container. Closing the bottle, he rotates on his toes, and stops dead to squint at something in the path leading up from the stream. Then he takes out his phone to shine a light into a deep depression in the soil and take some photos.

"Good lord," he exhales quietly. "That doesn't look like bear tracks to me." Standing, he spots several more moving away from the water before the ground is solid and overgrown enough that they don't show up very well, but trampled undergrowth leads away in the direction they're heading.

Miguel traces the outline in the ground and Good Boy goes over to inspect the hole for himself . The indent resembles the shape of a giant seed pod with a hooked stem reaching out at one end. It's so long that he could just about stand inside it. The smell in it is definitely of the creature that knocked him into the woods like he was made of leaves when Shriya and the other men were captured by the giant monkeys.

Good Boy, tries to imagine exactly how big the animal that could leave such a footprint would be and he doesn't like what he's picturing. Whatever left this would have to be larger than the bear he and Calypso had seen on the Pablo's magic window, unless those fish they catch are as big as dolphins! Now he would prefer it to be a mere jaguar.

Good Boy looks carefully in all directions and listens for movement, but only sees food critters and birds. One thing he's sure of is that, if this thing finds them, one man with a machete and a gun won't be enough even if they see it coming. At least he knows that the monster that hit him was big enough that his defeat at its paws is nothing to be embarrassed about. Most importantly, now Good Boy knows they've passed the point where Shriya was taken and he hasn't smelled any human blood. At least not yet.

The going is easier once they get up the embankment, as the path is raised slightly above the surrounding forest floor and the undergrowth is trampled into the topsoil from traffic, but that same exposure puts Good Boy on high alert. Miguel slips his gun off his shoulder to hold it at the ready and Good Boy is glad to see he feels the same way. The bugs swarm around them, but mostly stay off, thanks to the terrible smelling spray Miguel has put on them. Too bad it doesn't also repel monsters, or Shriya wouldn't have been captured. All Good Boy's thoughts stop suddenly as he picks up the scent of human blood and his own runs cold. In a panic, he follows his nose in a zigzag pattern over the ground before plunging into the jungle off of the path.

"Where's he going?" Juan Manuel asks Calypso.

"Don't you smell the blood? Follow him."

Juan Manuel jumps down an old path, overgrown, but recently trampled through. If they weren't following Good Boy's nose, he would think he was only following some deer or free goats who had passed through a few sky fires back. Good Boy runs ahead, but they catch up to him in a small clearing where he stands motionless on the opposite side about five goat lengths away.

"Don't come over here!" Good Boy warns them, too late.

"Oh," Calypso says. A bloodied body, covered in flies, leans against a tree. "Is that a person?"

"Yes," Good Boy says with a bit of relief over his worry, though a bit of anger is rising that will overpower it all. "A man. At least, it was."

"Blech!" Juan Manuel exclaims, jerking his head away from the scene.

"Good. I mean, that's terrible for this one," Calypso says with unconvincing sympathy, "but I'm glad it's not Shriya."

"Me, too," Good Boy agrees, casting his nose around to make sure that's the only dead person. "But, this one was with us when we were attacked."

Miguel stops behind them and scans carefully around the clearing with his rifle before approaching Good Boy and crouching down to him.

"Is there anyone else, boy?" Good Boy closes his mouth tight and stares in his eyes. He hopes Miguel understands.

Miguel takes off his boonie hat and swats some of the flies away from the body. The wounds show that the man has been stabbed by a large knife or a sword or something else long and strong enough to have gone completely through his chest. From as far back as he can stretch his arm, Miguel reaches into the dead man's pockets looking for identification to see if it's Rondo, but doesn't find anything.

The swarm of hungry bugs becomes intolerable, so he backs away from the body. Turning and shining the phone light reveals drops of blood on the ground leading back to the path. Taking another look around the clearing, Miguel sees that the path continues past the tree. His eyes land on Good Boy, whose own scan ends at the same time. They nod at each other and Miguel stands, looking around carefully before setting off down this new path. Good Boy frowns at Juan Manuel, who nods in solidarity.

"That was gruesome," he says to Calypso.

Good Boy decides to follow Miguel, and Juan Manuel takes up the rear.

"All young trees in this part of the forest," Calypso observes.

"Mm, yeah," Juan Manuel agrees.

"It's not just the path, it's the whole area. Doesn't seem like new growth after a fire."

"No, I don't smell old fire." He nods to a large tree stump, then another. "Chopped."

"Must have been people," Calypso says disapprovingly.

Ahead of them, Miguel stops and presses a foot on and off the forest floor. Good Boy puts his nose out to smell for danger, but doesn't detect any. Miguel crouches down and clears some of the soil and old leaves away to find a sheet of metal links extending underneath. Pulling on it brings up a small patch of jagged edges where the links appear to have been broken off from a larger piece. He furrows his brow and takes another look around, his eyes coming to a sudden halt over his left shoulder at an enormous bulging metal cylinder covered in young vines protruding like a small knoll with its lower end partially sunken into the earth. Pivoting on a toe to the source of his curiosity, his eyes register the outline of something that is not a natural form through the foliage of the near line of young trees. Good Boy matches the angle of Miguel's head to the large knobby cylinder and he carefully goes over to it. Metal, oil, and fuel—it smells of machinery.

Juan Manuel comes up and chomps on some of the leaves of the vines, but soon stops. "Not very good. I wonder if it's the rock they're growing out of."

"It's not a rock, it's something made by people," Good Boy says.

"An airplane engine." Miguel breathes in awe, standing over the friends.

"See?" Good Boy says.

Miguel puts a hand on one of the large cylinders that protrude from the central engine block like the arms of a star. A propeller blade is anchored into the ground and two more stick out to the sides, unbent as if waiting for someone to dig them out. He grabs onto the most horizontal blade and tests it with his weight. It doesn't move.

Curious, Calypso clamps a claw around its leading edge, then taps it, and then smells it. "This smells like the thing that the animal in the box turns to make the boat go. I don't know where the animal is." She sniffs around some more. "I don't think there's enough water here for a boat."

Good Boy paws a cylinder that is pointing toward the ground.

"What makes the boat go isn't an animal," he says, "it's one of these . . . things the people make."

"How does it work?" Calypso asks.

"I have no idea."

"It's too big," Juan Manuel adds.

"This isn't for a boat," Good Boy says, "it's for an airplane."

Calypso blinks. "A what?"

"The big birds the people make that they fly in."

"They fly?"

"Haven't you seen them?"

"No."

"They fly right over the trees all the time," Good Boy says. "They're loud. They make a constant droning sound."

"Those are birds."

"No, those are made by people. There are people inside of them!"

"How do you know?"

"Miguel just said it's an airplane engine."

Calypso slowly nods her head. "When?"

"Just now!"

"Oh, I wasn't listening. How do you know about airplanes?" Calypso asks.

"From the magic window."

"This wasn't a crash!" Miguel says loudly from where he has walked a few meters away.

Miguel pulls himself up through the open rear doorway of a largely skeletonized airplane fuselage being colonized by climbing, twisting vines, and shadowed by some fast-growing trees that have already grown above it. A monkey runs out from a hole where a window had been and a squadron of parrots fly out from a gaping void in the top, chattering and squawking. Miguel ignores them all, stepping into the debris-filled interior, and keeping a careful eye out for hostile animals who don't like trespassers.

The cabin has been stripped out except for some expanded metal dividers large enough to hold people separately from each other. Something runs along his right leg and he looks down at a two-meter long constrictor snake. He stumbles back in surprise, catching himself on one of the dividers before falling. The disinterested constrictor continues to the cockpit area and Miguel hops back out the side door to the ground.

"Snakes," Miguel says. "There are snakes hiding in there."

Good Boy cautiously approaches Miguel and the plane. Juan Manuel follows. "This was an airplane," Miguel holds out his arms like wings. "People flew this in the sky."

He points up, but the animals just stare at him.

"It didn't crash. It was landed." He stomps on the ground with his heel. "There was a makeshift runway built here." He nods and looks around. "Probably cartel, but I don't know what they'd be doing way out here, or why they'd abandon it. I wonder if these were prison transports that were hijacked to free whoever was . . ."

Miguel notices another abandoned aircraft in a similar state of decay through the initial forest overgrowth.

"There's another one! These planes look like they've been here for quite a while. Lot of missing pieces, like someone's used them for parts, which is odd. Maybe there are local people living around here that stripped them. Or maybe they're the ones who killed that guy."

"How does it fly?" Calypso asks Good Boy.

"It doesn't. This one is dead and its wings are gone."

"Now birds live in it. I like that."

Miguel walks past them, back toward the trail, before turning around and clicking and waving for them.

Juan Manuel and Good Boy follow after him.

"I wonder why it didn't eat him," Calypso says as they pass the dead man again.

"Why didn't *what* eat him?" Juan Miguel asks.

"Whatever killed him. Don't predators only kill to eat? I thought only people killed for other reasons."

"What about bears? Good Boy said there was a bear."

"I don't know. Maybe. Or maybe it was other people that killed him."

Good Boy takes a last look at the dead man, snorts, and passes Miguel to lead them back to the trail with all his senses on high alert and looking for a reason to attack.

"If you thought that dead person was terrible to see, you're definitely not going to want to watch what Good Boy will do if anything happened to Shriya." Calypso says quietly.

"If anything happened to her, I'll be right there with him." Juan Manuel says, with a snort.

29

When they get back to the main trail, Miguel notices old blood leading in the direction they're headed. "That guy might have been trying to escape whatever we're heading toward," he says to the animals, then frowns at himself. He hopes they can make it somewhere safe to set up camp before nightfall.

Banging, shouting, and hollering ahead stops Good Boy instantly. The smells of the giant monkeys and the monster bear roll in strongly—especially the monster—and does it ever smell! Miguel crouches down and scans the woods, sweating fear. Calypso looks up to the trees and contemplates making a climb for the canopy while there's still time. Juan Manuel wonders if he can outrun Miguel and Good Boy. On the clear ground Good Boy is probably faster, but definitely not Miguel. Juan Manuel doesn't have to be the fastest, just not the slowest. Sorry, Miguel! He wonders if Calypso could hang onto his collar tight enough to stay on and notices that there's another path cleared out on the right. Good Boy has also noticed it, looking back and forth, wondering if they should try it so that they'll be less exposed. He nods to himself and leads everyone down the new route.

They move as quietly as possible, but the noises seem to be getting closer. A heavy crack pierces through the forest from back up the path, then more cracking and the rush of crashing foliage, ending with a thump that the friends feel through the ground.

Miguel thinks they might have run into illegal loggers poaching protected trees and that some kind of truck or construction equipment cleared that path. He wonders if they built the airstrip for the planes, too. He pauses and scratches his head, not knowing how they could have fit heavy tree harvesting equipment in those planes, or how else they would have got them here, or gotten the trees out. He checks his phone to confirm he has no signal and looks at his rifle as if it were a squirt gun—if Shriya and the rest of them are still alive, he's going to need an army of police to rescue them from poachers. They'll need to wait until the poachers leave and go back for help.

Good Boy growls quietly—he knows it isn't people because he had seen the big monkeys and caught a glimpse of a giant monster and he smells them both now.

"The trees," Calypso says to Juan Manuel. The branches are stripped of leaves reaching to about the height of several people, and she can smell the sap from the wounded tree where the bark has been torn into.

"What about them?"

"Come on, we need to go back!" Miguel says, patting Juan Manuel to get his attention, but the friends only look at him.

A low rumble like distant thunder shakes the air, then a spooky howling, "*Ahhoooooooooh*," followed by a strange sound like the mix of a dog bark and donkey bray clipped off at the end that fills the space between the trees. The animals of the jungle go quiet for a few moments.

Good Boy looks at Juan Manuel and back toward the sound.

Miguel's face goes white as he realizes they're not dealing with poachers.

Good Boy growls at smelling Miguel's fear and determines it's on him to try to deal with the bear. Calypso reaches out for the trees, but they're too far away.

"*Ar! Ar! Ar!*"

The sound grows closer, coming from the raised path not far off enough for any of their comfort.

Good Boy and Juan Manuel, with Calypso still on his back, look at each other and rush down the new path, hoping it leads them far away from whatever is behind them, but it ends at a clearing around another cave with a round opening tall enough that Juan Manuel could barely hit the ceiling with a running jump. Miguel catches up and takes out his phone, which he uses to light up the cave. Then, holding the rifle up to his right shoulder, with his left hand holding the barrel of the rifle steady and the phone's light between his fingers, he leads them inside.

The cave is filled with the stale foul smell of the monster. Good Boy sneezes as if to force out the pungent stench that threatens to burn through his nose and Miguel switches to breathing from his mouth, but it's so strong he can taste it. The smell is like the most noxious possible mix of skunk, rotting meat, and animal musk unlike anything he's smelled before.

Calypso closes her eyes and shakes her head as if she could evade the odor. "This is a bad place."

The cave forks to the left and right. Miguel turns left and goes down a short distance until the odor is so strong that it makes him dizzy. Figuring it's either a dead end or occupied with whatever it is that smells so badly, he turns around, and the light illuminates the stone cave walls covered in long gouges and scratches. Touching them, he's horrified to imagine the size of the claws of whatever dug out this cave and he runs the light to the ceiling to see that it is frighteningly high.

"We need to get out of here," he says just as the terrible stench increases, becoming so strong that it overwhelms him, knocking him to his knees, gagging for air. The light clatters to the floor and lands pointing at the ceiling. Thunder rumbles through the cave.

Good Boy growls and barks into the darkness, putting himself in front of Calypso and Juan Manuel. "Get back! Get back!"

"I'm with you!" Juan Manuel stands fast.

"No, get her out of here!"

"There's nowhere to go! It's you and me, like the time when we saved that captive sloth."

Calypso slips off of Juan Manuel and crawls into the dark to hide, which seems like a better strategy than fighting, but they don't have the option. "OK," Good Boy says, "you go high, I'll go low. Get ready!"

Juan Manuel lowers his horns and hops up onto his hind legs.

Another low rumble reverberates and echoes off the stone walls, vibrating their bones. A heavy humidity envelops them.

"Uh oh," Juan Manuel groans.

"It's a giant bear!" Good Boy barks, backing slowly away. "Watch its claws!"

Miguel gathers as much breath as he can and points his rifle in the direction of the thunder. A giant, furry beast with a body that almost fills the cave roars at him, blowing off his boonie hat. Juan Manuel and Good Boy dodge the swipe of a massive claw before falling to the ground, gasping for air from the stench, Miguel fires a shot. The noise in the confined cave stabs their ears and the flash from the gun reveals a human-like figure leaping toward him from beside the monster. The gun is torn from Miguel's hand in the darkness, but he's able to pocket his phone just before he passes out.

## Kukulcan City

     Roused by the fresher air outside the cave, Miguel, Good Boy, and Juan Manuel are forcibly walked back to the path by a couple of large chimpanzees holding spears. The beast lumbers behind them on the sides of its feet with an awkward gait, and a third chimpanzee rides its back, pulling reins to direct it like a horse. The path soon widens and passes under an ancient corbel arch with the anchors of cleared vines still apparent on the stone surface.

     Beyond the arch, the left side of the road is lined by forest barely kept at bay by a fence made of reeds taller than a person. To the right, an open field continues the length of a long football pitch to more forest. Two chimpanzees cut back the vegetation overgrowth using scythes with blades of obsidian attached to a wood backing. Ahead, and surrounded by a field, a massive Mayan-style step pyramid, cleared to bare stone with flights of steep stairs up the center of each of its four sides looms above them. Some distance behind it on the same side of the road is a second, smaller pyramid, looking much like a hill, being still largely covered in soil and vegetation. Past the reed fence, a large dirt berm is bisected by another road that extends perpendicular from the main road they are on. Part of a thatch-roofed hut peeks out from behind the more distant berm, smoke rising from that area, accompanied by the noises of animals.

     The rider of the giant beast slides off its back and releases it to cross the field to the tree line, where it stands on its hind legs to pull vegetation off the branches and vines with its long tongue and into its mouth. The horrid smell of the monster is immediately replaced by that of cooking meat and vegetables, which reminds Good Boy of how hungry he is.

     The friends are walked by the road between the dirt berms and Miguel sees that it is an old ball field, the stone walls lining its sides being well preserved. Hooting and laughing drifts back from ahead. Beyond the thatch hut, along the road they are on, a group of chimpanzees are stripping a large log of its limbs and bark with some well used steel tools.

They are stopped at the hut and prodded to turn down a new road running parallel to the old ball court. Several chickens peck around for insects at the edge of the dirt and Good Boy wishes he could peck around for chickens, though at this point, he'd even have what they're having. One goat in a fenced in paddock, sees them and turns away, two more stare at them without expression, and a last goat bleats out a warning, but there's nothing Juan Manuel can do.

The road is lined with round thatch dwellings on the right and a long series of wood-column stalls on the left, with the missing large airplane wings on top, forming the roof structure. Smoke from cooking food wafts from some of the stalls and several chimps arrive at one of them with various vegetables and animal carcasses in bags suspended along the sides of a donkey, which they begin to unload.

They pass another stall with a line of spears leaning against a horizontal pole. One chimp sits on a chunk of log, striking a jagged black stone with a rounded gray stone to break off flakes in order to form spear points, while another in back uses a stone-bladed axe to rough out a wood shaft from a cut down tree branch.

Juan Manuel nearly trips over Good Boy, who has stopped with his nose pointed at one of the food stalls. One of the chimps screeches at them and the club end of a spear shaft swishes through the air. Good Boy apologizes to Juan Manuel and they are all pushed past the closest hut and between the next two. Behind the neat row of huts lining the road is another field with even more huts scattered about in a haphazard manner.

A waiting chimpanzee guard stands in front of a hut where the round exterior wall is a cage made of stripped tree branches lashed together with twine. Good Boy barks in excitement. His nose has recognized Shriya in the nearest hut! The guard opens the door and Good Boy runs to Shriya who greets him with open arms, followed by Juan Manuel. Miguel is shoved inside. Good Boy barks at the chimp guard as he closes and latches the door.

"Miguel!" Shriya stands and embraces him.

Shriya then bends down and hugs and pats Good Boy again as he jumps up on her and licks her face. She hugs Juan Manuel too.

"How did you find us?" she asks, with her hand still on Juan Manuel's head.

"Buca showed up and I knew something was wrong, so I went to your place and found your notes and the LiDAR photos had the coordinates written on them," Miguel says. "I'm glad he came to the boat in case I needed him for his nose. Charleston insisted on coming along, too."

Juan Manuel snorts, "*He's* the one who insisted on coming along!"

Shriya rubs the sides of Good Boy's head affectionately. "I can't believe he made it all the way back through the jungle after we were captured. These animals are incredible!"

"Yeah, I'm finding that out," Miguel agrees.

She stands up and nods to the other man with them. "Miguel, this is Rondo Julius, he's a friend from university. He sent me the photos. Good thing, too, it seems."

"Hi, how are you?" Miguel asks with a hint of uncharacteristic coldness.

"We're trapped in the jungle by some kind of advanced chimpanzees, so . . . I've been better."

"Right, so what is this, what's going on?"

Shriya answers, "Last year, a plane carrying rescued lab chimps to a sanctuary disappeared and was never found. We're pretty sure these are the survivors. I don't know where else they would have come from and, if you look around, you'll see scavenged airplane parts that don't look like they were in a crash."

"I found the skeletons of two planes overgrown by young trees and vines in the jungle just outside this place," Miguel says. "The wings were missing, but there was no crash—the planes were landed there. I found some temporary runway material like the cartels might use. Why would someone leave them here? They must have chosen this place for a reason, don't you think?"

"It would be an odd coincidence to leave them in a random spot that just happens to have been an ancient city," Rondo says.

"We think they killed the pilots and crew," Shriya adds.

"Why do you think that?"

"There are human heads on poles in front of the large pyramid. Well, they're just skulls at this point."

"I didn't notice them," Miguel says, swallowing hard. "What are they going to do with us, then, eat us?"

"They've been making us help them to turn this place into a livable city again," Rondo explains. "As an archaeologist, I know a lot about primitive technology, so I've been able to tell and show them how to build things. They learn surprisingly quickly."

Shriya wrinkles her forehead. "The zip lines aren't so primitive."

"*Mostly* primitive things," Rondo insists. "I want to know where they found those zip lines. I can't imagine there's any kind of adventure tourist spot near here, but if there is, we might be able to get some help."

"I want to know why you helped them set them up for use on lookout towers," Shriya says.

"That wasn't me, the chimp king thought that up."

"Chimp king?" Miguel asks.

"Yeah," Rondo says, "he seems to be the main decision maker and the other chimps go to him. He also mediates their disputes. He'll be around. He's somewhat friendly, though I don't know how much of it is just that we're useful to him."

"How do you tell them apart?" Miguel asks.

"Once you've spent enough time around them," Shriya says, "you can tell them apart."

Rondo adds, "The king wears an airplane propeller spinner like a crown, but I think it's more so the other chimps can spot him from a greater distance than for status."

"Did you show them how to make this village?" Miguel asks.

"No, most of this was already here, and the large pyramid was cleared off. Unless the missing pilots and crew showed them what to do, I think they figured it out themselves. We don't know where their animals came from or who trained them to work with them, either."

Miguel frowns and looks at the guard. "I knew chimpanzees were supposed to be smart, but I thought they barely used sticks. These are crafting spears and building cages and lookout towers."

Rondo nods. "And making fire and cooking, too. Makes you wonder what kind of experiments the lab was performing on them."

"You think they were making them smarter, like *Planet of the Apes* or something?"

"I don't know. Maybe it was some kind of advanced teaching lab."

"But what if they did? The chimps don't talk, do they?" Miguel laughs nervously. "How are you talking to them?"

"They speak ASL," Shriya says.

"I didn't know you knew sign language," Miguel says.

"I took ASL as an elective at university."

"What did they tell you about why they're keeping us?"

"They only tell us that as long as we help them, we'll be fine." Shriya raises her eyebrows in doubt.

"That is not very helpful of *them*. So, they need us?"

"For now."

"Speaking of communications," Rondo asks, "do you have your phone?"

Miguel checks his pocket and pulls out his phone. The light is still on from the cave, so he shuts it off and checks for signal bars, then sighs. "Nothing. Battery charge isn't doing so well, either."

"I didn't think so, but worth a shot."

"If only I hadn't lost the satellite phone," Rondo laments. "But at least I got the big battery!"

"So, you found the sloth," Shriya says to Miguel.

"Uh, yes. Well, *these* two did," he answers, gesturing at Good Boy and Juan Manuel. "They showed up with him. I don't know what happened—he must have gotten away in the cave when we were captured. I passed out from the smell of that beast."

"No, no," Shriya says, "the beast in the cave is the giant ground sloth. Wait, are you saying that Calypso was here with you?"

"Giant sloth? I thought it was some kind of bear! Those aren't extinct?"

"Not so *ex*tinct, but it definitely stinks! It's probably either a descendent of Eremotherium or Megatherium. The range would match the ancient range of the Megatherium, but a lot of things can happen in eons."

"As funny as it sounds, that smell is no joke."

"Yes, it's *really* bad. So, Calypso? Calypso is a *she*, by the way."

"That's the little sloth that you taught to drive the speedboat?"

"Yes, but I didn't teach her to do that. Where is she?"

"She must be back in the cave. We heard that giant sloth coming down the main trail and ran into a cave where we were captured," Miguel says. "The last I saw her, she was riding the goat, so I think she must have climbed off and hid."

Shriya sighs and looks toward the rainforest reaching up above the top of the fence. "That wasn't a cave, that was the giant sloth's lair. I hope she's ok."

"She's probably better off than us. How did she learn to drive the boat if you didn't teach her?" Miguel asks.

"She must have learned from the guy she lived with originally. It was his boat."

"You told me you got the boat cheap, but you never told me it came with a sloth!"

"Nobody would believe a sloth piloting a boat unless they saw it."

"That's true," Miguel nods.

Rondo sticks his hand between them. "So, wait, some guy taught a sloth how to drive his boat? I don't even know how that's possible, have animals spontaneously gained higher intelligence?! But this guy also sold you the boat cheap and gave you his pet sloth? Was it to be your chauffeur? I need to hear this story!"

Shriya sighs. "I never met the guy who owned the boat, but his name was Pablo Rios. From what I could put together, he was a smuggler of some sort and I imagine that's what got him murdered."

"How did you know he was murdered?" Rondo laughs. "Did the sloth tell you?"

Shriya glares at him. "I looked up the boat registration, which gave me his name, which led to a news article about his murder. After doing some more investigating, I ended up getting in contact with his sister, who happened to be here from the United States to deal with his estate. She came to my place to see the animals. That's how I found out the sloth's name is Calypso and the dog's name is Bucephalus, though I just call him, *Buca*."

"How did the goat get his name?" Miguel asks.

"His sister never knew he had a goat, so I call him Charleston, as in Charleston Chew candy because, well, he's a goat. Funny thing is that he doesn't chew everything like most goats. He's very well behaved."

"I hate that name," Juan Manuel says to Good Boy, who agrees that the name doesn't sound right.

"What's the dog's full name, again?" Miguel asks Shriya.

"Bucephalus."

"Weird name. Sounds like Greek or something to me."

"Alexander the Great's horse," Rondo says.

"What?"

"It was the name of Alexander the Great's horse. Alexander named a city for him in what is now modern day Pakistan after the horse died, likely killed in battle. He was very fond of that horse."

"Hm. Strange name for a dog, though."

"He *is* a trained protection dog," Shriya says.

"He is?"

"Those are expensive!" Rondo adds.

"Yes. And I think maybe he got his name because the sloth rides him like a horse." Shriya says.

"Are you saying the sloth reminded Pablo of Alexander the Great, conqueror of much of what he knew of the ancient world?" Rondo asks.

"Maybe it was meant to be funny. I mean, the guy was obviously some kind of a character—a smuggler with a speedboat that's a little small and slow for offshore use and the usual kind of smuggling work."

"That boat is a good size for traveling up narrow waterways," Miguel says. "You know, for secret meetings or to escape more seaworthy boats.

"That's a good point. He could have just been some kind of local delivery guy," Shriya agrees. "That still doesn't explain its other oddities, like being set up with a stick control and a sliding canopy like a fighter plane that you can't close in the sun without becoming a baked potato, or why he taught a rescued sloth to drive."

"Or how! That boat sounds interesting, too." Rondo says, pausing for a moment. "*Calypso* is also Greek. She was a nymph who kept Odysseus enchanted on her island for seven years. Funny thing is, the name means, *to hide*, like, in a deceptive manner. If sloths do anything well it's hide. Sounds like this guy was either Greek, or really into the mythology. Not what I would expect of a smuggler, either."

Shriya shakes her head. "People are more than their work. I only met his sister, but I don't think he was Greek. Maybe his mother was, but he obviously didn't have a Greek name."

"There's also calypso music. That's not Greek," Miguel adds.

Rondo nods at him dismissively and looks at Shriya. "I wonder how a smuggler ends up with a sloth."

"His sister told me Calypso's mother was killed by dogs when she was not quite old enough to be on her own, but some neighbors saved her, and Pablo took her in. I don't know why the neighbors gave her to him, but Bradypus sloths are known for being difficult to care for, especially when they're young, so he must have found out what he needed to do and made her a high priority."

"Yeah, that's not the kind of guy I think of when I imagine a smuggler," Miguel says.
"Maybe he was an animal lover and was just doing what he had to do to get by." Miguel frowns and cocks his head, "He couldn't find anything legitimate to do?"

"Everyone has different strengths, Miguel, I wouldn't do it, but I *couldn't* do it. I know smuggling and looting usually go hand-in-hand, and that I should hate looters, given that they destroy clues about ancient biology and the environments ancient animals lived in." Shriya stands and steps up to the bars of their prison, looking to the pyramid. "They're not all that far removed from poachers, but I didn't live his life. What I know of him, he doesn't sound like such a bad guy. Maybe he did some bad things, or maybe he just broke some arbitrary laws and stepped on the wrong toes, but whatever it was, an evil person wouldn't have saved a baby sloth."

"I understand, but it just seems strange. Those guys are usually super macho, and I wouldn't think taking care of a baby sloth would fit with that."

"Maybe that's why he was killed," Rondo offers, "the people he worked with thought he was weak."

"Whatever it was, why did this guy teach the sloth how to drive the boat?" Miguel wonders again.

"I guess we'll never know." Shriya says, turning back around to face them.

"His sister gave you the boat, then?" Miguel asks.

"Well, not exactly, but she only wanted three thousand US to sign it over to me in exchange for looking after the animals. It had some damage, but not enough to make it that cheap. I think she just didn't want to deal with it in the short time she had to take care of everything else, and she wanted to cover her costs and make sure the animals were taken care of because they meant so much to her brother."

Juan Manuel aims his ears at some commotion coming from the market street and wonders if the big monkeys could have captured Calypso, but he can't see anything. "Do you think Calypso is still back at the cave?" he asks Good Boy.

Good Boy takes a moment to answer, mind occupied by observing the area trying to come up with a plan. "I hope she found her way out by now. She's not here, so either they didn't catch her or they didn't bother. Whichever it is, that's their mistake."

"What could she do to help us? It would take her a bundle of sky fires to even crawl here and if the people haven't figured out how to get out, what could she do?"

"I don't know, but at least she's not stuck in here."

"What about Calypso?" Miguel asks Shriya. "You didn't have her living with you."

"No. She might have lived with Pablo, but Bradypus sloths don't do well in captivity and the rescue center checked her out and said she was fine to go back into the wild, so I put her in the wooded area where there aren't any people, roads, or power lines nearby."

"Power lines?" Rondo asks.

"They don't insulate power lines down here, so electrocution is a big problem for arboreal animals that climb onto them."

Rondo nods. "There are so many little things I take for granted in First World countries, but I never even would have thought of that."

"Buca seemed to know where Calypso was," Miguel says.

"Yeah, I'm sure he did." Shriya shakes her head, "I can't get over them—I don't think anyone's ever seen anything like it. They're simply unbelievable!"

Miguel nods his agreement, but then asks, "I don't understand. If you got the boat before you got the animals, how did you know she could drive? How did you find the boat in the first place?"

"They found me. I was heading out for a boat ride when the old engine on my Zodiac decided to quit in the strongest current at the mouth of the river, so I looked around for someone who might be able to help and saw a nearby speedboat. I waved my arms furiously, like I was trying to guide an airplane into land. When it pulled up, I saw it was occupied by these two, plus two male sloths with Calypso driving."

"She had herself her own little harem, huh?" Miguel laughs.

"What's a harem?" Juan Manuel asks Good Boy.

"I don't know. I think it was a joke to mean she had rescue sloth and Drunk Monkey to mate with."

"I don't get it, but I guess I have a harem of goats."

"Yeah."

"Not you, though."

Good Boy sighs, sits, and stares at him, "I'm aware."

"I didn't mean it like that. You're always welcome at the herd . . . if you can dodge Mace!"

"Thank you, but I'm a dog's dog."

Shriya narrows her eyes a little. "No, one of the males was in really bad shape. I think they rescued him from somewhere because his claws were clipped and he had a torn string tied around him that might have been used to tether him to something. I had the sloth rescue come and get him and they were able to nurse him back to health. They planned to release him if his claws grew back, but they often don't grow back straight enough to use. They had hope, though, since they said it looked like it was mostly just the outside of the nail that was damaged. See, their claws are bone, but covered in keratin, like our nails or hair are made out of. They said the other male was fine, so I released him with Calypso in the same place."

"Growing back crooked sounds almost like reptiles that lose their tails," Rondo says.

"Kind of. With their slow metabolism and inability to regulate their body temperature, sloths have a lot in common with reptiles." Shriya pauses and looks over at the two friends. "So, Buca and Charleston showed up at my house with Calypso?"

"No, first Buca got Charleston at my place and when I came out to go to them, they ran off. I figured that something must have happened to you on the expedition and Buca must have made it back through the rainforest, so I went to your place to get the notes you left to see if I could figure out where you might be. I had my emergency bag and some food in the truck that I threw in the speedboat before I went to get your notes. Then, as I'm locking up the house I see the animals stealing the boat and I had to run down the dock and jump for it. I almost missed," Miguel shows the bruises on the undersides of his arms where he hit the boat.

"Oof, that looks pretty bad."

"It's OK," he laughs. "At least they helped me in."

"This is a real story?" Rondo asks with a frown and furrowed brow, touching his hands to his temples.

"Completely."

"This is the most amazing thing I've ever heard! So, the sloth doesn't just know how to drive the boat—because that's not crazy enough—it can get it started and everything?"

"Oh, yeah, she can even tie it up to the dock!" Shriya says. "I mean, not perfectly, but good enough to hold if the water is calm."

"And untie it?"

"Yes, and untie it."

Rondo scratches his captivity beard. "I didn't even think sloths were smart, never mind able to learn such things!"

"It's not like they get a lot of stimulation with their lifestyle, and their senses are pretty limited, so they don't usually have much opportunity to learn or varied experiences to draw from," Shriya says, after a minute. "Pablo obviously exposed Calypso to new things that constantly engaged her mind in ways wild sloths never have to. Of course, I also doubt that she's of normal intelligence." She nods to Good Boy and Juan Manuel. "All three of them are rather exceptional."

"Maybe they'll be able to think of a way out of here," Miguel says, "because I don't see one."

"Yeah, we need all the help we can get," Shriya agrees.

"Maybe the missing sloth with come to our rescue!" Rondo laughs.

The chimpanzee guarding their cage bangs the bars to get their attention and signs something at them.

Shriya translates for Miguel. "He's saying that if we try to escape, we'll be killed."

"He understands us when we speak, then?" Miguel asks fearfully.

"It seems so."

Miguel sighs and sits down on the dirt floor. "So, did I pass a ball court on the way here? I thought the Mayan cities had a ball court where they played a game that was similar to football and basketball, using decapitated heads for balls?"

"We don't know if this place is Mayan," Rondo says. "It has some similarities, but it's out of their known territory and would take some study to really determine who built this. As to the games, from what we know about it, it was more like hacky sack, where they had to keep a solid rubber ball—not heads—from touching the ground without using their hands."

"So, what was the hoop for?"

"If anyone got the ball through it, that was an automatic win, but it probably wasn't often attempted, since it was so difficult to do and a missed attempt would make it all the harder to prevent the ball from hitting the ground." He nods in the general direction of the court. "The dirt mound that makes up the rear of their market street is the back of one side of the stands of the ball court. I told the chimps what it was for and they seemed to like the idea, but so far, they haven't been using it."

"And, they haven't killed anyone yet, except maybe the pilots?" Miguel asks.

Rondo frowns. "We came here with two guides. They escaped, but they were pursued, and the chimps came back fairly soon. The guides weren't with them and I don't think it's because the chimps gave up and let them go."

Miguel takes a deep breath. "We found a dead man against a tree, just off the trail and not far from the giant sloth's cave. Looked like he'd been stabbed with a sword."

"Or a spear?" Rondo offers, looking at the chimp guard.

Miguel follows his eyes. "Yeah."

"Did you see a second body at all?"

Miguel shakes his head, "No, but did either of them have cross earrings?"

"Enrique."

"The man we found had cross earrings."

Rondo nods solemnly. "He was a good man. Never seemed to let anything bother him too much."

"He was funny," Shriya adds, her eyes darkening with anger as she clenches her teeth. Good Boy picks up on it and puts his head on her lap. She pats him absently.

"I'm sorry," Miguel says.

Shriya rubs Rondo's shoulder.

Changing the subject, Miguel nods toward two chimps walking by on their way to the market street. "It looks like some of the chimps have gray hair. Are they old?"

"I have no idea, but they don't act old," Shriya says, grateful for the shift. "Could be from stress, or something that was done to them."

Miguel watches the chimps disappear around some huts. "I always thought chimps were smaller. And I thought they mostly walked on their knuckles."

"Neither of us are chimp experts," Rondo says, "but yeah, they don't walk on their knuckles much. Chimps get pretty big, though. They usually only use young ones in the movies because they get too big and dangerous when they're older."

"Makes sense," Miguel nods. "At least that's *something* that does. I feel like we're in a weird dream." He watches as a line of chimpanzees command a small army of donkeys and goats to drag large tree limbs out of the forest behind their prison hut. Following them is the giant sloth with a chimp on its back, slowly dragging a massive tree trunk with the help of chimps placing and replacing logs underneath it to use as rollers.

"Where did they get all the animals?" Miguel asks.

"They must have come on the planes or maybe there's a village or farm or something not too far from here that they raided," Rondo says. "I didn't see anything on the Lidar surveys or the satellite images, but they could be outside the survey area hiding under the forest canopy."

"Maybe there *was* a village near here and they just killed the people."

"Yeah, we thought of that, too."

"Something is going on," Juan Manuel says to Good Boy, looking at the top of the pyramid.

Good Boy pulls away from Shriya to look where Juan Manuel is, but he can't see much at that distance. "What is it?"

"There's a chimp—"

An archaic sounding trumpet blares from the pyramid's peak, provoking the workers to stop and look toward it. A chimpanzee stands at the top, shaded by tree branches held by attendants, a shining silver metal cone on his head glinting in the sun. He hands an animal horn off to an attendant and signs

48

directions to other chimps who relay them down the pyramid to the workers on the ground. The giant sloth is prodded to pull the tree forward until it runs off of the rolling logs and he is unharnessed from it and ridden around the far side of the pyramid. A team of chimps half drags and half carries a large semicircle of dried vines and ropes to the center of the tree, rotating one leg over the top of it. then tipping it up, and extending out a series of half-hoop framework tied together along the tops and sides by rope down the length of the tree like the skeleton of a bellows. As each semicircular frame is put into place and held vertically, another pair of chimps pound stakes into the ground near each leg, tying them to the stakes while another team works on weaving leafy tree boughs between and upon the ropes to create a kind of tent structure over the tree. To support the structure, the horizontal ropes extend past the end frames where they are secured by stakes that look to be nearly a meter long pounded in at angles facing away from the tent. The chimps use a wood tool to tension the ropes far beyond what they could do by arm and hand alone.

"These cannot be ordinary chimpanzees," Miguel marvels.

"I agree. I taught them a lot of that, but the smarter ones learned it quickly and they taught the others." Rondo says, turning to the pyramid and gesturing to the top. "That's the one we call their king."

"He's more of a thinker than most of them," Shriya adds. "If we get out of here, I think it will be by being friends with him."

"Maybe *you* can," Rondo says. "He really likes you."

Shriya frowns at him. "Are you implying that I'm attractive to apes?"

"Man, ape, what's the difference?" Rondo shrugs. "Besides, you see any female chimps here?"

"It couldn't be that he likes me because I'm the one who can speak ASL, though, could it?" she asks.

"That was supposed to be a kind of self-deprecating joke comparing men to apes," Rondo explains, "not an insult."

"Stick to archaeology," Shriya says, not amused. "I'm not attracting anyone after a week with my only shower being rain storms."

Miguel slaps his knee. "You know, I remember hearing about that plane crash on the news now! Was it some kind of—" he stops to look up toward the source of a swooshing, zipping sound. The chimp king hangs from a carrier sliding rapidly along a cable that stretches from the top of the larger pyramid to the ground on the side closest to them. Several more sets of cables reach from a raised pole like a mast in the center of the upper platform of the pyramid leading to three look-out towers that sit just within and above the canopy trees at the outer edges of the city. "Are those ziplines at the top of the pyramid coming from the look-out towers?"

"Yes," Rondo says to him. "Originally, I thought they must have traveled through the jungle before getting here and stolen most of the parts from one of those jungle adventure tours, but you said you found some airplanes nearby, so I'm thinking someone left them here on purpose."

"How would they know about this city?" Miguel asks. "And why would anyone leave the chimpanzees here?"

"As far as I know, nobody else knows this is here except for a few of the guys I work with, but the chimps have obviously been here for a while," Rondo says, "probably since that plane was reported down or maybe these are from different planes altogether."

"And how did the chimps know how to dig the wells and make the huts?" Shriya adds. "Did someone train them and leave or were they killed?"

A crashing noise comes from the area near the pyramid, drawing the guard's attention.

"Did you bring your rifle?" Shriya asks.

"Yeah."

"We had one, too."

"So, you think it might be because we had guns with us that—"

"*Ar! Ar! Ar!*" the monster sloth shouts from the direction of the crashing noise. A clatter follows, chimps screech, a donkey cries out, a goat shouts angrily, and the noise follows to their side of the pyramid where the sloth emerges in a strange kind of gallop.

Hearing the distressed goat, Juan Manuel looks toward the direction of the noise. A goat flies through the air and crashes down only a short sprint away from where the chimps are working on the tree tent. The workers leap aside as the goat lands on top with a crack, then rolls off the top into a kicking, rolling heap that sends leaves fluttering into the air.

The giant sloth lumbers over to it with the chimpanzee on its back pulling ropes tied to its limbs to command the beast. The sloth sniffs the badly injured goat, who tries to rise, and the chimp pulls a rope for the sloth's right arm. Juan Manuel bleats a hollow threat that's ignored and the sloth rumbles like thunder, standing on its hind feet taller than any animal Juan Manuel has ever seen. It shrugs as if it wants to throw off the chimp, who holds fast, jabbing the sloth in the back with a sharpened stick. With a roar, it smashes its enormous clawed hand down on the goat. Juan Manuel turns his head away. A chimp runs over to grab the dead goat, putting it over his shoulders, and carrying it toward the main street.

"Certainly not like the gentle sloth that drives the boat," Miguel says gravely.

"They changed a lot in adapting to the trees," Shriya says.

"It's also got a face more like one of those big deer they have in Canada than a cute sloth," Miguel says.

"Do you mean a moose?" Rondo asks.

"Yeah, a moose."

The giant sloth looks at them briefly as it turns around to go back to the field behind the pyramid.

Good Boy approaches Juan Manuel, who is trembling with anger. "I think the people are saying that's not a bear, but some kind of massive sloth," Good Boy says, horrified.

Juan Manuel pauses for a moment. "That's completely ridiculous. Wait until Calypso hears—if she doesn't like the creatures she calls tree pigs also being called sloths, she *really* won't like sharing a name with this one!"

"Yeah, but look at the claws and how it walks. Maybe it *is* a giant sloth."

"That doesn't mean it's a sloth," Juan Manuel says. "I have a tail. You have a tail too, but you're not a goat."

Good Boy frowns and watches the scene.

"Do you think Calypso will grow that big?"

"No, I'm pretty sure she's full grown." Good Boy says. "Maybe it's just like how there are small goats and big goats like you."

"Yeah, but we all look like goats. That thing . . . are you sure it isn't a bear?"

"I'm not sure of anything."

"What a horrible monster!" Miguel exclaims. "I wish they really were extinct."

"I think it just wants to be left alone," Shriya says. "That's probably how it's survived all this time. The chimps are controlling it and they use it to maintain order, but it certainly doesn't appear to like it."

"But why bother with that thing when it smells like it does?" Miguel asks. "Adult chimps are pretty formidable without that creature *and* they have spears!"

"We wondered that, too," Rondo says. "We think because they were controlled in a lab from a young age, maybe they don't realize their strength. Or they could have just found the sloth living nearby and happened to recognize that they could use it to intimidate everything."

"And it can drag those big trees they're using to build with," Miguel says.

"That, too."

"You think that lab might have been experimenting on the chimps with some kind of intelligence boosting?" Miguel asks.

"Could be. As smart as chimps might be, these really seem to be especially, peculiarly smart. And brutal," Shriya says.

"Wild chimpanzees are pretty brutal," Rondo says. "They have wars and will kill and eat the opposition's children."

"Then maybe it's just our shared nature," Shriya halts her breath, and looks at Rondo. "The city, the airplanes, and the sloth—that's three coincidences!"

"What are you saying—the people that might have set the chimps up here also knew about the sloth?" Rondo asks.

"No, I'm suggesting that maybe they *made* it."

"What?!"

"These chimps came from some experimental lab. They are especially smart—like us—they walk upright—like us," Shriya explains. "What if they're the result of some genetic hybrid experimentation?"

Rondo puts his hand to his forehead in disbelief, then disguises it by wiping off sweat. "You're talking about recreating a giant extinct sloth. Even if they could get intact genetic material and could generate an embryo from it, what animal would they use as a gestational carrier?" He scratches his beard, thinking.

"I don't know how small their young are," he says, "but an elephant is about the only thing I can imagine that would be large enough to work and they can't possibly be genetically close enough that the elephant's immune system alone wouldn't destroy it."

"I'm not saying that's what happened," Shriya says, "I'm just throwing out an idea while trying to make sense of all these very strange coincidences. The other option is that it has survived in a rainforest in secret for thousands of years, where they originally lived in open grassland, and left no fossils behind in the last ten thousand years."

# Kingdom of the Apes

The chimp king approaches their cage with two attendants behind and to his sides. The guard steps aside and the king signs for him to open the door. Then the king points to Juan Manuel and signs to Shriya.

Shriya says and signs back, "*No, he is our friend, not food.*"

The king nods, seemingly satisfied, and motions for them all to come out and walk with him. They follow him past the backs of the huts to the main street that leads through the gate. Some of the chimps look up from their crude wood working to hoot and point. A few appear to laugh. They walk past the pyramid and turn right into the old ball field. Its long sides of carved stone walls are twice as tall as Juan Manuel. Above the walls, the sides are gently sloped grass and on top of the slopes are flat areas where a few goats and donkeys graze. He motions for them all to sit in the shade from one of the walls and he sits down next to Shriya and puts the propeller spinner crown on the ground next to him, rubbing his head. Juan Manuel eats some vegetation that clings to the stone wall.

She can see now that the base of the spinner has thread woven through holes punched into it, holding a cloth layer inside where it sits on his head. Good Boy pushes himself between them and the king shuffles over a little to make room. Good Boy points his nose ahead, but keeps his eyes on the king. Three chimps arrive carrying food on plates of woven dried reeds and places them down in front of the king, the people, and Good Boy. The food is various roasted fruits and meat. Good Boy scarfs down the meat immediately. The king looks understandingly at Good Boy and nods to dismiss the food attendants. The guards that came with them remain standing on each of their flanks

Finished with the meat, Good Boy starts to gnaw on a bone when he suddenly notices Juan Manuel staring down at him. "How is it?"

"Really good! I was starving so much I could eat a skunk!"

"Or a goat?" Juan Manuel asks accusingly.

Good Boy drops the bone onto the plate, horrified. Shriya takes the bone off of his plate, adding it to the bone on her plate, and petting his head, "You can't eat rabbit bones, they'll splinter."

Relieved, he casts his eyes up at Juan Manuel who blows a raspberry at him and walks back to eat the vegetation along the wall. "Do you want my fruit?" Good Boy asks. He gives him a moment, but he doesn't respond, so he eats that, too.

The king signs to Shriya, who translates for the others.

"*These are your friends. They came to get you?*"

"*Yes.*"

"*How did they know you were here?*"

"*I knew there was a cave here. The cave was supposed to be empty. Did not know chimpanzees were here. I drew a map to the cave and left it at my home. Miguel, this man here,*" she points to Miguel, "*found the map and followed it here.*"

The chimp king considers this for a moment and then signs, "*Why you come to find bear cave?*"

"*As I told you before, it is a giant sloth cave. I study animals like the giant sloth, so I wanted to see it.*"

The king scowls. "*Other people find map?*"

"*No, the map is here with us,*" Shriya signs as she shakes her head. "*There is no other map. No more people will come here.*"

The king looks doubtful. "*People come here. People bring us here. More people have map.*"

Shriya waits a moment, then takes a chance, asking, "*What people?*"

"*People in people bird bring us from bad place with few trees.*" The king looks sad as he signs.

"*The laboratory?*"

"*People place. I don't know what is called.*"

Shriya feels bad for the king and his chimps, but she also wants to understand, so she asks, "*What happened to the people who brought you here?*"

"*Those people die.*"

"*Did you kill them?*" Shriya asks.

"*No.*" The king shakes his head. "*One die from sickness, other die from L-I-N-D-O.*" He spells out the word and makes a special sign for it.

"*What is Lindo?*" Shriya asks, using the special sign.

"*Other chimpanzee.*"

"*Why did he kill him?*" Shriya asks. Miguel and Rondo look at the guards warily, but remain silent.

"*No like people,*" the king grunts. "*Most chimpanzee no like people.*"

"*I understand,*" Shriya says. "*I don't like a lot of people, either.*"

The king makes a face like he's laughing, without sound. "*Why you not like people?*"

"*They kill many animals, kill each other, do terrible things.*"

"*We kill animals to eat,*" the king says. Shriya wonders if he is testing her.

"*Yes, but you don't kill all animals,*" she says. "*Animals I study are extinct. Many of them were most likely killed by people.*"

"*What means that word?*"

"*All dead, no more of those animals alive anywhere,*" Shriya explains. "*Sometimes the animals cannot adapt to change, sometimes they cannot adapt to people.*"

He nods. "*How do people know all animals dead?*"

"None seen anymore," Shriya signs.

"*How you know not somewhere else?*"

"*People check every place the animals were known to live.*"

He looks doubtful again. "*How you study if all dead?*"

"*We study bones found in dirt and things they left behind, like caves,*" Shriya tells him, her hands flying.

"*Why you do this?*"

"*I find them fascinating,*" she signs, "*and learning about what happened to them can help people to understand how to adapt to the environment changing and maybe stop forcing animals extinct.*"

"*Why environment change?*" His face grows confused and concerned. Shriya thinks she may be going down a dangerous path, but continues.

"*Climate changes happen thousands of years apart, but today, people are causing the change to accelerate.*"

"*How they do this?*" the king asks.

Shriya shakes her head and pauses, unsure how to explain such a thing succinctly. "*Too many people making too many changes.*"

The king grunts and holds out an arm, palm up. "*People stop changes.*"

"*People are too stupid.*"

The king looks away for a few moments before turning back. "*Big sloth is alive.*"

"*Yes, people thought they were extinct,*" Shriya agrees with him. "*We are wrong about that one.*"

The king looks at her, and then signs, "*People know.*"

"*People know what?*" she asks.

The king waves his hand at Shriya, Miguel, and Rondo. "*People know big sloth alive.*"

"*Yes,*" Shriya agrees, "*but we are the only people who know.*"

Chimps yell from the street behind them. The king stands and looks over the ballcourt wall. Juan Manuel stops chewing for a moment out of nervousness and one of the guards starts to climb the wall when the yelling stops and he returns to his position flanking the king and company.

Sitting down, the king furrows his brow and signs, "*No, people know.*"

"*What people?*"

"*People from bad place. Big sloth from bad place.*" The king glares and his fangs show. *People bring big sloth here, too.*"

"Whoa." Rondo says quietly to Shriya as she translates this to him and Miguel. "You were right!"

"Well," she says, "we don't quite know they made it."

"What else would it be?"

"I don't know." She returns to the king.

"*Do you know why people bring you all here?*"

"*To build city,*" he signs.

"*Why would they do that?*"

"*Don't know,*" he shrugs like a human, "*People show us how to do things, bring us here, and leave us.*"

Shriya considers this and then asks, "*Is good that they leave?*"

"*Not all people leave,*" he laughs again, silently.

"*We are not those people,*" Shriya insists.

The king scratches his head before continuing. "*People leave. Very difficult to live here without help.*"

"*We are helping you,*" Shriya says. Rondo nods.

"*You show us, but work is still hard.*"

Shriya waits a moment, then says, "*I'm sorry it is this way for you.*"

The king shakes his head. "*This way for everything. Sneaky cat eat small animal. Small animal no like to be eaten, not easy for sneaky cat to get. Sneaky cat need to eat or die. Same for all. Maybe not same for people.*"

"*People kill people,*" Shriya says, "*and not because they want to eat them.*"

The king nods thoughtfully. "*People kill everything. People eat too much!*" he laughs.

She just smiles back. "*Are there any other giant sloths?*" He shrugs.

"*Did you see any other giant sloths at the bad place?*" she asks.

"*No.*" The king looks down the field toward the empty entry road. "*Big sloth all alone. Big sloth sad. Some chimpanzee say hear other big sloth in forest. But only one sloth in bad place. Only one sloth here.*"

Shriya decides to chance pushing him a little. "*Sloth probably does not like being poked by rider with stick.*"

"*He does not,*" the king nods. "*But we need big sloth to help pull trees for city. Need stick to make sloth help.*"

"*That sounds like people excuse,*" Shriya says. Miguel puts a hand on her shoulder as a warning, but she ignores him.

"*We people chimpanzee,*" the king signs.

"Do you think he means they're hybrids?" Rondo asks.

Shriya shakes her head. "I think he's just acknowledging the similarity."

"Ask him," Miguel suggests.

"*Do you mean you are part people?*" she signs.

"*Not people, chimpanzee.*" He rubs the hair on his arm.

"Maybe he doesn't understand," Rondo says. "Ask him if they're partially human."

"Do you want to try to explain genetic engineering to him?" Shriya asks in annoyance. "That level of technology shouldn't even be possible for *us.*"

"Ask if they're born by females or where their babies come from," Miguel encourages her. "Maybe that could give us an idea."

"They'd still have to be gestated in a carrier even if they're engineered!" she says.

"Who knows with the kind of tech we'd be talking about. Besides, you see any females here? What if they use human carriers?"

Shriya puts a hand to her head. "That's a terrifying thought."

"Ask him!"

"Fine." She turns to the king. "*Where do your babies come from?*"

The king laughs silently again, rolling on his butt and slapping his leg. He gets the attention of the attendants who are watching for trouble and signs her question to them. They join in the laughter.

Rondo frowns. "I take it that they're using chimpanzee carriers, if that's even what's going on."

The king stops laughing and nods at her belly, "*Where do people babies come from?*" Good Boy watched carefully, smelling a slight whiff of fear on Shriya at this.

"*Yes, it's the same, but you are not like normal chimpanzees. We are trying to understand if you are not true chimpanzees.*"

The king shrugs. "*People call us chimpanzee. People word. Chimpanzee not care.*"

"I don't think he's getting it," Rondo whispers.

"Yeah, that's fine," Shriya says to him. "Maybe we could try again later when I can think of a way for him to understand. For now, I'm glad that he's being friendly."

"Maybe it's not a good idea in the first place," Rondo says, thinking this conversation has gone on long enough. "First thing, he's unlikely to know, but second thing is that if they are hybrids, they might get the idea that they can mate with us."

"Me, you mean," Shriya says. "As you said, I haven't seen any females here."

"And that's a whole lot of monkeys!" he laughs.

"One is too many, thank you." Shriya says. Good Boy can see that Shriya is not amused and he barks at Rondo. Shriya laughs and pets his head.

"I think I saw one in the market area," Miguel says, "But I wasn't really paying attention to that at the time."

She nods. "You might be right. They don't take us through there."

The king taps her shoulder. "*What saying?*" he signs.

She thinks fast. "*We were wondering what the bad people have done to you in the laboratory and where the females are.*"

"*Bad people keep us locked in small space.*" He pokes her with his finger and Good Boy barks and growls teeth at him. Shriya puts a firm hand on the back of Good Boy's head to calm him down and the king pulls his finger away.

"*Dog no like me!*" he shakes his head and pokes his own arm with a finger. "*Bad people stab chimpanzee through skin, scare chimpanzee, hurt chimpanzee with lightning stick.*" He nods.

"I am sorry they did that to you," Shriya signs "Are there females here?"

The king leans back and smiles, eyes brightening, pointing to himself. "*Sneaky. I know what you say to people.*" He does his silent laugh again. "*Females here in huts, in market. Females make stuff, cook, will take care of babies.*"

"*You have babies here?*" she asks.

"*No babies. Maybe chimpanzee doesn't know how babies made,*" he grins, his fangs showing again, "*but chimpanzee keep trying.*"

Shriya turns to the two men and gives them a knowing frown. Rondo scowls and nods and Miguel looks confused, so she silently mouths 'sterilized' to him. Miguel raises his eyebrows in understanding and sympathy.

"*Bad people also teach chimpanzee how to live like people,*" the king continues. "*Don't know how to live like chimpanzee. Where other chimpanzees?*"

"*Chimpanzees don't live here,*" Shriya tells him, "*they live across great ocean in continent of Africa.*"

"*What is continent?*" the king asks.

"*Huge land.*"

The king's brow wrinkles and he looks into the distance, pondering for a moment. "*How far?*"

"*Very far.*"

He thumps his chest. "*Chimpanzee build boat.*"

"*It would have to be a very big boat with room for all chimpanzees,*" Shriya signs. "*and a lot of food and water on board.*"

He scratches the top of his head. "*How many days travel?*"

"*Many weeks if you can build a big enough sailboat that can handle the ocean and know how to navigate,*" Shriya says.

He narrows his eyes, processing the thought. "*You teach.*"

Shriya puts her palms up in alarm. "*I don't know how to make a boat.*"

He points to the men.

She laughs, "*Definitely not.*" Rondo and Miguel look offended, but she doesn't care.

The king laughs, too. "*Chimpanzee should not have pulled people bird apart. Chimpanzee fly there.*"

"*People bird is called 'airplane',*" Shriya says, and repeats the sign.

The king copies her and nods.

"*Very hard to fly airplane,*" she continues, "*and airplane would not be able to fly so far.*"

"*Airplane fly far to get here,*" the king insists.

Shriya shakes her head. "*Africa is much farther and airplane needs fuel. No fuel here.*"

"*What is fuel?*"

Shriya thinks for a moment. "*Water that burns. Comes from thick black water very deep underground. People change it to make light fuel.*"

"*You make?*"

"*No, I don't know how. Needs very big buildings and tools. No oil here or else people would be here to get it.*"

"*Bad people not teach us, either. Bad people not want good people and chimpanzee to know.*"

The king's last comment hangs in the air and everyone is silent for a moment as the other chimps clear away the remains of the meal.

"Pretty damn smart," Rondo says. "I mean, it's not that simple, of course, but that's really insightful. If they're not hybrids, then we're really underestimating their cognitive abilities.."

"We're not," Shriya says.

The king swallows the last of his fruit and signs, "*What does he say?*"

"*He says what you say is very smart.*"

The king thumps his chest again., "*That's why other chimpanzee follow.*"

Shriya asks, "*So, the bad people taught you how to do all this?*"

"*Some teach before fly here, some after come here. People came with us not bad. Lindo should not have killed. Lindo no like people.*"

"*We understand how he feels after the bad things they did to you.*"

He nods.

"*What is your name?*"

"*Chimpanzee call me Papa. Means father. I am like father to all chimpanzee.*" He strikes his chest and looks around. Juan Manuel catches his eyes. "*No eat goat?*"

Juan Manuel tenses and Good Boy stands up.

"*No,*" Shriya signs sharply. "*That goat is our friend.*"

He looks her in the eyes for a moment. "*Some goat friends, some goats food. Some people bad, some people friend. Lindo not—*" a riot of noise explodes from the market street behind them, cutting him off. "*You go back to hut. Papa fix problem.*" He sighs, putting the cone back on his head and signing to the attendants to bring them back to the holding hut and stay with them. Deftly gripping the cracks between the stones, he scrambles the few meters up the wall, and the attendants lead everyone else back to their hut.

On the way to the hut, they hear hooting and screeching from the market street. Looking down the street, chimpanzees are standing off against Papa and about a dozen loyal followers. Two females scramble around the four and come around the back of Papa's crowd. Good Boy barks a threat, smelling the violence in the air. Papa's attendants push them all past the street to with nervous urgency.

Just before the huts block his line of sight, Good Boy spots a large chimp calmly evaluating the situation from the top of one of the airplane wing roofs. He barks a warning to Papa, but he either doesn't hear or understand. After guiding them into the hut, the attendants secure the door and sign for them that they are safe, but Shriya feels they're saying that to assure themselves rather than their captives. Good Boy is at full alert and Juan Manuel stands behind him, ready to follow his lead in case they have to fight.

# Thundersloth!

The cave is cold, smells terrible, and it didn't seem like they had gone that far into it, but while having to haul herself back along the floor, it seemed to have no end. Finally, though, Calypso sees the outdoor light that marks the entrance, dimming with the ending of the day. If she can get up a nearby tree before the sky fire goes out, the reduced light might help her to find where the giant monkeys and the smelly monster bear took her friends. If not, she might be able to follow her nose.

At last!—past the cave entrance and out in the warmth and fresh air. She smiles and takes a deep breath to clear out the smell and—oof!—why does it still smell so bad?! The ground shudders and she looks up to see the monster trudging in her direction with surprising quietness in spite of its size and the awkward way it walks on the sides of its clawed hands.

She freezes in place hoping to be mistaken for a fallen nest or something, but it's too late  The monster stops and looks directly at her. She can smell now that it is a male and she looks directly at him as he reaches out with his nose to sniff her. She holds still in spite of the terrible stench that makes her eyes water. With a sniff of curiosity, the beast pulls his head back and turns slightly to get a closer look at her with his left eye.

Able to breathe slightly better with his head pulled away, Calypso lifts one of her arms threateningly toward him in the hope of scaring him off. Instead, he moves a massive clawed hand to her, its intimidating hooked blades almost half as long as her body. He pokes at the sunglasses on top of her head, so she gives him a slap as hard as she can. The hard clack of her claws on his seems to startle the beast and he withdraws his arm to look at her hands. They oppose each other in a silent standoff until Calypso feels he's unlikely to hurt her. She decided to continue crawling for the closest tree before he changes his mind.

The monster follows her with his head the whole way, and watches her climb. Almost out of energy, fear provides her with some extra strength and she does her best to pretend he's not there to get up the tree as fast as possible. When she's a few body lengths up, the giant bear blocks her with a claw large enough to not just pull fish out of the water, but dolphins. She turns to him and he moves his arm down to her height.

He looks up into the tree and back at her, then touches her arm gently, as if offering to help her up. It must be hard to make friends when you smell so bad, she thinks. Deciding to trust him, since he could easily have killed her if he wanted to, she climbs onto his arm. The beast stands on his back legs, lifting her far up to the branches of the tree. She climbs off him onto a tree limb. Looking back and seeing her own claws up close with the monster's claws well behind, their similarity from such a perspective strikes her—the claws, the beast's awkward walk . . . it occurs to her that he isn't a giant bear. He's an enormous sloth! What kind of leaves does he eat? she wonders. The giant drops back to the ground and looks up at her,

"*Ahhoooooooooh!*" he cries out.

"*Aaaahhhhiiiieeee!*" she responds with a wave.

The giant snorts in satisfaction and nods to her, turns into his cave, then looks back one last time. None of the strange-smelling, people-sized creatures that were with him when they took her friends are anywhere to be seen, so she starts to climb again. A growl of thunder comes from the cave and she looks down to see a small animal scampering out at top speed, its frightened screeching telling her it's a monkey.

Just like her, he doesn't like monkeys! Luckily, the monkey takes a different tree than hers and Calypso continues climbing, thinking that maybe the creature that was with the giant sloth was one of the giant monkeys Good Boy was talking about and that those things are the whole problem. Giant monkeys, giant sloths, *noisy* giants . . . too many animals are larger than her! Calypso decides to come up with a new kind of name for the monster sloth. She stops to scratch her head and grab a claw full of leaves. As she eats, a name pops into her head: *Thundersloth!*

Utterly exhausted, Calypso reaches the top of the tree by the last light of the falling sky fire and is pleased that her tree is one of the tallest around, though it's not the very tallest. No, the tallest tree she can make out is in the direction they had been heading before they ran into the cave. It's an odd tree, or perhaps it's just her eyes, with a curiously squared growth of branches near the top that form some kind of box shape unlike any tree she has seen before. The branches above the box are absent, leaving only the very top of the canopy intact, reminding her of a person wearing a hat. It's not too far away for a goat, a dog, or a thundersloth to get to, but very far for her.

Beyond the strange tree, the canopy seems to end, telling her that there is either a cliff or that the forest thins into a clearing like the people have around their dwellings. If she could get Thundersloth to help her, she could get in there, and maybe the two of them could get her friends, but she suspects that he's afraid of the giant monkeys and wouldn't be able to help.

She picks out some tender new leaves with her nose and eats them—she needs a plan, but first she needs to know what she's dealing with. Night is the best time to travel, but it'll have to come after she rests, and that will probably take until after the sky fire rises again. She eats some more before finding a nice protected spot where three branches meet to curl up to sleep.

The rising sky fire wakes Calypso, who yawns and climbs up for another look at the unusual tree before it gets too bright. Mouthing more leaves while studying, she realizes that what she thought was the top of the box-like growth of tree branches is actually the railing of a fence with the floor of a platform just beneath it. She's only ever seen people make fences on the ground to mark their territories. Is she seeing a tree or is that ground? No, it must be a tree!

Something moves within the fenced-in area. After a long stare, she concludes that it might be a person. With a long blink to clear her eyes and help her limited vision see a little better at the distance, Calypso thinks it could also be one of those giant monkeys. Below her, Thundersloth wakes up in a bad mood. She watches him exit the cave with a rumble and a grumble. She waves to him, but he doesn't notice.

Two giant monkeys step forward, aiming spears at him while a third gets on his back the way she rides Good Boy and Juan Manuel. Now she's sure that the figure behind the tree fence is another giant monkey. The rider monkey pulls some ropes and Thundersloth and the two other monkeys head back through the forest in the direction of the platform tree. One friend at a time, she thinks, pulling down her sunglasses to counter the increasing light of the sky fire. After the cold of the cave yesterday, the warmth that comes with the light renews her energy, and she returns her attention to the strange tree.

Another giant monkey climbs up to the platform and jabbers briefly with the first monkey, then the first monkey reaches up to the stripped trunk that rises above the middle of the platform and grabs something with its hands. It leaps over the fence and glides down somewhere beyond the trees. Calypso scratches her head and chews more leaves. No wonder Thundersloth doesn't just squash them—there are many, and they can fly!

She spends time eating and wondering what it would be like to be as big as Thundersloth and able squash monkeys. Gross, she frowns, thinking about how she'd have to pick all the monkey guts from between her claws. Squashing anybody would be out, even monkeys. Of course, if they hurt her friends . . .

But if she was a thundersloth, she'd also stink. Would a thundersloth like their own smell? She should ask Good Boy, she thinks with a yawn. He stinks, too, if not nearly so bad. Enough hanging about. The foliage is dense enough here to make her way over without having to go to the ground, so she can eat as she plots her way through the branches to the platform.

## Pyramid of the Sun

Three chimpanzees holding sharpened spear shafts with no blades approach the guards, who raise the heads of their stone-tipped spears to them. The new chimps hiss and bare their teeth, and the guards hoot an alarm that doesn't seem to be heard over the cacophony still coming from the market street.

"Something's going on with these giant monkeys and I don't like it," Good Boy says to Juan Manuel.

"Nope."

"And I don't see the one behind the challenge to the conehead monkey."

"Shriya said he calls himself 'Papa'."

"Yeah, I know, but I'm sticking with conehead."

"Like the cones they put on the injured animals?" Juan Manual asks. "Don't they usually face the other way?"

"A conehead is a conehead." Good Boy growls.

"He might be our biggest friend here."

"We don't have friends here."

"I don't know about that," Juan Manuel says. "We have ones who don't want to kill us and these here, who look like they feel differently. How do you know which monkey is the problem?"

"Smell and I know when I see a power play," Good Boy says. "That I don't see the one behind it is what worries me."

"I'm worried enough with these."

The people are standing at alert, so Good Boy takes the bench to give himself a launch platform. "See, the people know, too," he says as he paces along the bench.

"Know what?" Juan Manual asks.

"There's a fight about to happen, and we're going to be in the middle of it."

Juan Manual blinks. "At least we're safe in here."

The smell of more chimps, of fear, and anger comes from the tree line. Good Boy's eyes follow his nose and his confidence falls to the ground. "Goat, we're in a kill zone."

Juan Manuel's eyes focus on the trees and his blood runs cold. "What do we do?"

"Get by the door. We need to get out of here!" He barks poison darts at the trees.

Miguel, Shriya, and Rondo turn and follow Good Boy's pointing nose toward the darkened forest.

"You see anything?" Miguel asks.

"No," Shriya says, "but I'm sure there's something there."

"I wonder if it's that chimp Papa mentioned starting a coup." Rondo says.

"Lindo," Miguel says.

Five chimps burst out of the forest and one guard swings his spear at the three challengers in front of him while the other one opens their cell door.

Juan Manuel turns to the people. "We're having monkey for dinner. Get ready," he says, followed by a low, guttural groan. They don't know what he said, but they understand the point.

Miguel points to four additional chimps with wood spears who are rushing from the forest. "Four more!"

"Do you think we can outrun them through the woods?" Rondo asks.

Miguel shakes his head, "Only if they forget about us because they're fighting each other."

The two guards hold off the other chimps by swinging and jabbing their spears, screaming for help.

"These two guards won't last long," Rondo says.

"Here comes back up!" Shriya announces.

Good Boy tenses, looking for an opening through the short legs of the guards who have backed themselves into the hut to protect their rear as the new force crashes into them. A parried spear enters the hut, which Miguel is able to catch with his foot and jam against the bars. The spear comes loose from the chimp's hand and Miguel pulls it inside.

"Brilliant!" Shriya yells as Miguel flips the spear around and jabs at the attackers. A war cry rings out from the market street—Papa and a dozen allies rush toward the fight. Renewed by the coming reinforcements, the guards push the attackers back, clearing the swing of the door and Good Boy takes his opening, flinging it open with his snout, Juan Manuel right behind him.

Miguel follows with the spear to face the attackers. A chimp catches Juan Manuel's horns under his chin, screaming, and falling flat onto his back. They're all targets to him, but Good Boy scans the melee and immediately finds one, leaping up and locking onto his arm in midair, using his weight to spin him to the ground. Shriya grabs the chimp's free arm before he can use it to smash Good Boy and the powerful chimp throws her off, but Miguel stops him permanently with the spear to his chest.

Miguel yanks the spear from the dead chimp and goes for another, but his target scrambles to his hands and feet to leap-frog out of his reach. Good Boy mauls another chimp, who then receives a crack to the side of the head from Juan Manuel's horns. Shriya picks up the dead chimp's spear and swings it wide to break up a charge from two more attackers. Papa charges his way through the dissolving line of rebels, and Good Boy moves to chase the retreating chimps, but Rondo grabs his collar. Papa and his troops rush past in pursuit.

"Dammit, run, run, run!" Rondo shouts to everyone as the chimps leave them behind. They all make a break for the main street. With Juan Manuel leading the charge like a battering ram and Good Boy running zigzag protection from pursuers at the rear, the friends are about to pass through the city gate when three chimps leap from between the stone pillars and block the road. They try to get around, but are soon encircled by spear points. A small monkey pelts them with things from the trees as the sound of thunder comes up from behind, followed by a smell that even makes the chimps cough.


-------------------------|||-------/o) _ (o\-------|||-------------------------

Calypso nearly reaches the lookout platform in time for the chimp at the top to open a trap door in the bottom, drop a spear down the hole, and rush down the tree. Good Boy barks over the howls of far too many giant monkeys. Thundersloth roars and Calypso hopes he isn't hurting her friends. She's about to yell to him when she sees the giant monkey scrambling back up the tree.

She doesn't want to draw its attention, especially when she's not sure Thundersloth will even hear her, so she stays dead still as the monkey climbs past her and through the platform trap door. A wood latch rotates to hold the door closed and now Calypso knows how that works. The trap door creaks and shifts a little under the weight of the excited monkey walking across it and  hooting loudly at the action below.

An idea sprouts up in Calypso's head and grows like bamboo. At night, she'll be ready, but her friends will need to hold on until then. For now, there are some leaves nearby—not the best, but good enough—and a warm sun spot to catch up on some rest. She's going to need the energy. This is no kind of life for a sloth!

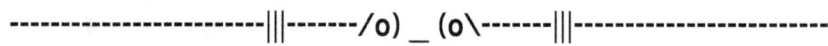

Good Boy, Juan Manuel, Miguel, Shriya, and Rondo are marched to the front of the large pyramid between the armies of the two factions of chimps. Papa and a usurper yell and sign across to each other. The usurper's army isn't as large, but is substantial enough for Papa to want to avoid fighting it out. Another chimp, the fur on his arm and the side of his face crusted with blood, steps up next to the usurper and yells.

"What are they saying?" Miguel asks Shriya.

"The bloody one is complaining about his injuries."

"Serves him right," Rondo says.

The usurper signs to Papa again and Papa signs in return. Back and forth it goes, rapid fire, and Shriya tries to keep up.

"They're negotiating. The chimp who's against Papa is ready to go to war and Papa doesn't want that. The losses would threaten their ability to survive. As I'm sure you've figured out, the usurper is, Lindo."

"No surprise," Rondo says.

"Lindo is willing to accept the one we killed and let us survive, but he doesn't think they should have to accept the ones who were injured by Buca and Charleston."

"What does that mean?" Miguel asks.

"I don't know," Shriya snaps, annoyed at the distraction, "they're still talking!"

"Alright, alright."

Papa turns to his guards and motions for them to take the people and friends back to the holding hut.

The sun comes up over a cacophony of animal noise as Papa and Lindo approach the hut with six guards armed with spears to add to the two who had kept watch on them all night. Immediately, the guards jam the spears through the bars, forcing Shriya, Rondo, and Miguel against the back of the hut. Three more reach inside to hold them from the back.

Good Boy growls and tries to bite through the bars of the door and one of the free guards raises his spear to stab him.

"Buca, stop it. Stay!" Shriya commands, and Good Boy complies, but leaves his teeth on display. The guard lowers his spear and Lindo opens the hut. With a swift move, he grabs hold of Good Boy's collar and grips him tight, holding him away from them, and preventing him from twisting his head around. A guard grabs Juan Manuel by the horns and pulls him out of the prison hut to Shriya's protest. The hut is quickly closed again as Good Boy and Juan Manuel are led away. Papa signs to Shriya that he's sorry.

"Sorry for what?" she asks.

He gives her the sign for sadness and that he's sorry again.

"Sorry for what?"

He steps away from the hut and the guards withdraw their spears from between the bars. The ones in back come around to the front and the door is opened again.

Good Boy and Juan Manuel are pulled by the guards toward the main street. The chimps debarking fallen tree trunks look up curiously, then put down their tools and cross over to the market street. Chimps in the shops stop what they're doing or shuffle out of their huts to climb ladders onto the embankment.

Good Boy and Juan Manuel are marched just past the market street, then forced to turn into the open end of the large rectangular field where they had sat down with Papa before. Today it looks more imposing and the grassy slopes above the walls are quickly crowding with chimps looking down at them or chattering with each other.

Armed chimps push Shriya, Miguel, and Rondo onto the grass in the stands in front of Papa. He stands and screams to get everyone's attention. The crowd goes quiet and turns to him. He signs something for the chimps and they cheer.

At the street end of the field, Thundersloth enters with no rider, roaring back fiercely at the chimps poking him with spears. At the opposite end of the field, more chimps jab Good Boy and Juan Manuel into the arena. Papa taps Shriya on the shoulder and signs, "*Papa negotiate peace with Lindo, save people, have to make animals fight because they attack Bando and Bando is very mad. Bando is Lindo favorite.*"

Shriya signs back, "*Why does Papa care about Bando? Lindo and Bando defy Papa, are enemies that will continue to cause trouble.*"

Papa sighs before signing his answer. "*Papa no care about Bando, care about peace. Cannot afford big fight. Lindo many chimps. Papa have more, but not enough. Big fight, many die. Papa no like chimpanzee dying and city cannot afford so many*

74

*dead. No worry about Lindo, jungle is dangerous place. Papa teach him one day."*

*"The Dog and goat are my friends,"* Shriya tells him, moving her hands emphatically without stopping to translate to Miguel and Rondo.

*"Papa know,"* he signs, then rubs his chest with one fist. *"Papa sorry."*

Shriya's defiant attempt to stand is thwarted by his powerful hand on her shoulder pushing her back down and holding her there. The guards behind her bang the ends of their spears on the ground. Good Boy and Juan Manuel are on their own.

The sky fire is emerging from its sleep and so is Calypso when the morning relief chimp makes its way up the tree to the platform. All but invisible in an adjacent tree, she looks on as the chimp climbs one-handed while carrying a curious contraption with a wood handle. A piece of metal dangles and clinks with every swing of his arm and feet as he scrambles from branch to branch up the tree. Calypso is impressed with his speed and hand placement.

The chimp reaches the platform and shifts himself over to hang on an angled brace connected to the tree trunk. He turns the wood latch that allows the trap door to open and pulls his arm back quickly as the door drops down to the outside of the platform to swing slowly back and forth at the end of its travel. He yells up through the opening at the night watch chimp, who yells back apologetically and lowers his arm to help him up.

The apes then pull a rope attached to the front of the door to lift it back into place and one of them turns the other end of the latch handle on the topside of the platform floor to secure it. There's some jabbering from the two chimps before it goes quiet.

A few moments later, the night watch chimp secures the handle contraption to a cable, takes hold, and rides down. The carriage and hanging chimp zip quickly out of Calypso's sight. She scratches her head and can't believe that giant monkeys could think of something so smart. But not too smart, she thinks, adjusting her sunglasses and making her way for the trap door.

The platform above Calypso creaks under the chimp's weight, the boards flexing around the supporting tree as he moves to scan the area. The door is above her and he's on the other side from where she needs him to be. She thinks for a minute and comes up with a plan she doesn't like, so she thinks some more.

Coming up short, Calypso goes back to her first plan and spends a little more time psyching herself up to execute it. Finally ready, she extends one of her arms from the tree to one of the diagonal platform braces that bracket the trap door and support the platform, then the other, and slowly climbs her way to the outer edge of the platform. Suspending herself from her feet claws and holding herself out fully horizontally, Calypso is able to hook her hands around the edge of the platform.

Feeling for a strong grip, the tips of her nails digging into the wood, she lets go with her feet and suspends herself from her hand claws, swinging slightly in the breeze. Reaching up past the floor, she feels for one of the platform's fence poles for a surer grip, and pulls herself up. The chimp is too busy looking toward the clearing, so she taps the floor with her free hand.

The chimp comes over to investigate as Calypso disappears back underneath. Carefully grabbing a platform support strut, she swings herself over and away from the opening arc of the trap door. The door shifts under the weight of the chimp and she gets a strong hold of a support strut and the tree with her feet and hand claws so she has the leverage to pull on the door latch with her free hand.

Claws biting into the wood of the latch opposite the pivot, Calypso pulls it toward her. It moves, but just a little, before sticking from friction with the weight of the chimp on top. She gives it another pull, but the latch stops and—curiously—turns back. She scratches her head and looks over to see the chimp's face staring at her from above the platform. It screams threateningly, its terrifying canine teeth freezing her with fear.

The chimp reaches underneath for Calypso, but she's lucky to be just beyond his grasp. If it swings over the side to come after her, she knows her only escape is to purposely fall, which is a very long drop, and he wouldn't be far behind climbing down, so she turns her brain on again and forces herself to remember all the dangers she's faced that were scarier than a giant monkey. The memories unfreeze her muscles and she reaches for the latch again.

The chimp pulls himself back on top of the platform, and with less weight on the latch, Calypso is able to turn it most of the way.

*Crack*! *Shoof*!

A chunk of the overloaded corner of the latch breaks away, dropping the chimp. "*Aaack*!" it yells, its clasping hands passing just by the end of Calypso's nose as it plummets through the open hole and tree branches, flailing for a grip of something on its long way to the forest floor.

*Crash, crash*! *Crack*!

Whomp.

Giant monkey is quiet now, Calypso thinks, blinking down at the blurry, waving foliage. The smell of chimpanzee dissipates and that of broken branches rises up. Patting the tree in apology before pulling herself up to the platform, there's a soreness in her left arm and she realizes the door must have hit her. It's still functional, so she presses on, but favors her other arm.

```
                /\     /\                          ~  \    /  ~
 ------------  \ 0`   `0 /  ------------------   (       )   ----------
                \   \/   /                           \_/
                 \/
```

In the death valley of ancient stones, the smell of the chimpanzees seems to roll down the grassy slopes to collect in the ball field. Good Boy tries to blow it out of his nose, then the wind shifts and the giant sloth's smell hits him like a truck. He prefers the chimps. "It looks like we're going to have to fight this beast and kill it before it kills us," Good Boy says to Juan Manuel.

"No, we're going to dodge it *until* it kills us," Juan Manuel says. "We can't kill that thing, it's as big as a barn!"

"I'm pretty sure it's a male," Good Boy growls, "and all males have the same weak spot."

Juan Manuel squints at the beast. "Are you sure? I don't see it."

"Remember the swimming sloth? They kind of hide them, but . . . it's there."

"I didn't really look, but I believe you. I still find it difficult to accept it's a sloth," Juan Manuel says. "What if that doesn't work?"

Good Boy raises an eyebrow to him. "Then you try to escape while they're distracted by watching it crush me."

Juan Manual steps back and shakes his head. "I appreciate the thought, but if we're going to be killed, it will be together."

"I'd rather have you at my side than anyone else," Good Boy says.

"Thanks, but I'd rather you have someone else by your side than me!" Juan Manuel answers.

Good Boy shakes his head with a toothy grin.

Juan Manuel paws at the ground. "But, if I'd never met you and Calypso, I'd have become some person's poop a long time ago. I've seen and done things that maybe no other goats have seen or done. It's OK. I'd rather be killed in a fight than led to slaughter."

Good Boy nods, "And now you'll be giant sloth poop."

"Nah,' Juan Manual says, "I don't think he'll eat us."

A thundering rumble rolls along the stone walls and down the field, vibrating their insides.

"*Ar! Ar! Ar!*"

Then a new sound, like the horrifying scream of a human in terror.

Juan Manuel steps back, "That's an awful noise. I thought he only *smelled* bad."

The giant sloth stands on his back feet and howls again.

"Oh, wow, he's . . . *really* tall," Juan Manuel says, rectangular pupils as large as they get. "I mean, I saw him before, but . . ."

"This is going to be like fighting an angry tree," Good Boy says.

"The kind of tree people could make a boat out of and —"

Good Boy interrupts his friend, "Does he have another mouth on his stomach?"

"Uh . . . no, I think that's just something on his fur that looks like a mouth."

"I really hope you're right," Good Boy says, eyes wide in fear.

"Does it matter?"

The giant sloth points its head into the air.

"*Ahhoooooooooh*."

"Oh, look!" says Juan Manuel, "He also howls like a dog. Sniff his butt and make friends so we can all bust out of here."

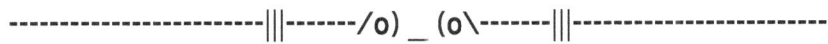

From the top of the tree that rises above the center of the lookout tower, Calypso can just about see what appears to her to be a tall, large hill sticking up from the clearing the giant monkeys come from. Staring for a short while, she thinks there might be another one behind it. Smoke comes up from the side, though she can't see what it's from. The smoke carries the smell of parts of animals and plants being burned, the way people prefer to eat them. Calypso wonders how the giant monkeys did all this. She's definitely going to need the help of Thundersloth to rescue her friends.

First she has to get down there to find them. Above her, rocking gently on the cable, is a carriage like the other chimp used to travel to the ground. Crawling to the edge of the platform, she tries to follow the cable to see where it goes, but her eyesight isn't good enough to make out where it leads, other than to the clearing below. Scratching her head, Calypso thinks that it still must be a better way down than a fall through the trap door. There's no other way for her to get there without a very slow and dangerous crawl that isn't an option. Putting her fear aside, she climbs the center pole to the cable.

Hanging from the cable just behind the carriage, Calypso smells the giant monkey on the handles that poke out from its sides, telling her that she needs to hang from there to use it. She tries to grab it like she climbed the cable, but letting go leaves her facing backwards and she's momentarily happy that it doesn't start down the line, only swinging side to side.

Suspended from the handles of the zipline carriage, her foot claws can just reach the platform fence rail, so she gets a grip on that to support herself to swap her hands on the handles and face the direction she should be heading. It's awkward and frightening as the carriage shifts with her, but with careful management of her weight, Calypso successfully turns herself around, which gives her a chance to inspect the carriage and figure out how it works.

Its main body is a block of wood with a handle sticking through both sides and extending far enough for even a giant monkey to hold on. One side has a plate made out of thick metal bent to support two pulleys over the centerline of the carriage. Poking at the groove in the pulleys and following them to the top of the cable, Calypso thinks she understands that it rolls on top of the cable with the rider's weight underneath stabilizing it, allowing for a fast travel in a manner similar to how she climbs under the branches of trees.

She's never seen a vine like this cable before—it's made up of hard twisted tendrils that her claws just glide right over. Picking at it, she finds that the vine is much harder than rope or the woody growth she's used to and she concludes that it must be something new that the giant monkeys made. With her claws locked tight around both handles, Calypso lets go of the railing with her feet, but the carriage rolls not more than the length of the end of her nose before stopping to rock side to side, leaving her hanging there.

She blinks a few times and wonders if she's too small to get the carriage to move, then turns her head around to see if there's someone holding it in place. The end of the cable is mounted to the protruding tree top that extends well above the platform and supports the canopy. A metal loop hammered into the tree below the cable holds a wedge of wood. Tied to the wedge is a thin rope Calypso had ignored before.

The rope leads to the back of the zip line carriage, holding it in place. Unable to get her claw into the knot to untie the carriage, she tries stretching her arm, but the wedge is out of reach, so she climbs the cable back to the wedge. Tugging on the rope attached to the wedge loosens it, but Calypso thinks she might be too far from the carriage to get back if she pulls it loose and it rolls away.

She scratches herself and hangs from the cable for a moment before climbing back to the carriage with a plan. Hanging from the handles, she twists herself around to grasp the wedge rope with one of her feet.

```
                    /\          /\                                ╲            ╱
 ---------------    \ 0       0 /     ------------------      ~  (      ╲  ╱      )  ~   ----------
                       \       /                                         \  /
                        \ V /                                            \ /
```

The discordant hollering of the chimps forms into an unintelligible chant.

"What do you think they're saying?"

Juan Manuel takes a deep breath, "Two friends enter, one monster leaves?"

Prodded by spears, the giant sloth turns to face Good Boy and Juan Manuel, "*Ar! Ar! Ar!*"

Good Boy barks a curse. "We should have attacked when it wasn't looking! How high can you jump?"

"I don't know."

"Can you hit him under the chin?"

"Not if he's standing up all the way," Juan Manuel says.

Good Boy nods. "We'll split the sides. If he charges down low, I'll draw him to my side and you hit him from your side as hard as you can."

"OK."

"If he raises up, hop around and try to avoid his claws, but draw him from me so I can attack his weak spot."

"Sure, that sounds easy," Juan Manuel says bitterly. "Just biting him will only make him mad, though, not beat him."

"I won't let go," Good Boy growls, the hair on his neck bunching.

"Love the confidence, but those claws are as big as my head—he'll tear you apart!"

"So, you just want to give up and let him squash us?"

Juan Manuel shrugs. "No, I'm just saying . . . it might take a couple of tries. I don't think we can just hit him once and he'll run away screaming."

"Understood."

A chimp strikes a whip that cracks near the ear of the giant sloth and the big animal lumbers toward Good Boy and Juan Manuel at an awkward, unmotivated gait. The chimps' frenzy gets louder and wilder.

When the beast approaches halfway down the field, Good Boy snarls, "Go!" kicking up clumps of dirt as his nails dig into the turf. Juan Manuel takes off for the opposite side of the field. The sloth stops short, almost falling over and swings its massive arms out at both of them, unable to connect, but disrupting their attack. As the crowd hoots, the chimps at the other end of the field lower spears at Juan Manual and Good Boy to prevent them from escaping.

They turn away from the spears, switching sides and stopping to rest while the giant sloth turns around and comes back. The beast snorts, stands up to its full height, and roars.

"New plan!" Juan Manuel pants.

"What is it?"

"I don't have one, I'm asking!"

"Uh, yeah," Good Boy says, " . . . try the same thing again."

"I said a *new* —"

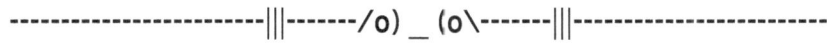

Preparing for launch, Calypso pulls the rope. It barely moves. Blinking in annoyance and thinking she might have to crawl down the cable to the city, she decides to give it another shot. This time grabbing the rope with both feet, she swings her whole body. Out pops the wedge, and the carriage starts riding down the cable. Just clearing the platform, the hanging wedge catches on the railing and jerks at Calypso's feet, but the string slips through her claws and the wedge pops off the rope before it can pull her off the handles, scaring her half to death and stopping her progress.

Luckily, when frightened, sloths freeze up. Now hanging in the open air, she contemplates how to climb the cable back without unbalancing the carriage when she shifts her weight, but the carriage starts to move again, picking up speed until she's going too fast to make sense of what's happening. Her claws are locked onto the handles like nothing she's ever gripped before and, even with her sunglasses on, her eyes water from the wind.

Calypso marvels at how she's flying like a harpy eagle and wonders how they make sense of anything at such speed. The termination of the cable at a large block on top of the steep hill suddenly looms up at her, rapidly increasing in size. Looking down, she's too high and moving too fast to drop off safely. Calypso braces herself, pulling up her legs just before impact, and letting go of the carriage at the last moment to—*boof*!

```
              / \     / \                    ~ \   / ~
-------------- \ 0    0 / -----------------  (       ) ----------
              \   /                             \_/
               \_/
```

Juan Manuel nods. "We've got him downwind. You should fart and show him he's not the only one with a secret weapon!"

"Wise remarks until the end, goat?" Good Boy asks.

"I will joke with my last breath," Juan Manuel says. "Though they may take my body and add it to rice, they will never take my humor!"

"I'd rather you help me fight."

"I can do both. I am—"

"Shh!" Good Boy growls, low in his throat.

"What?"

"Did you hear that?"

"*Ahhoooooooooh*!" the giant sloth calls over its shoulder.

"Yeah, so?" Juan Manuel says, "He's telling any vultures around to be ready."

"Not him," Good Boy says, "I think I heard Calypso!"

Juan Manuel stops short. "You think he's responding to her?"

"Maybe!"

"How would they know each other?"

"She was probably still in the cave when he went back and they must have met," Good Boy says.

"And she made friends with a giant goat-killing monster?"

"It's Calypso, why not?"

"I'm surprised he wouldn't just squash her," Juan Manuel says, "but OK, then how could she have crawled the whole way here without being seen? It's not like the chimpanzees would have let her ride the stink sloth in."

"Everyone underestimates that little sloth."

"Yeah, but it's not like she can fly!"

It takes her a moment to realize that she's stopped and not dead or even broken, just embedded in a thick pile of leaves and straw. Poking her head out of the bale and straightening her sunglasses, Calypso looks around  She doesn't see anyone. The carriage lays on the platform beneath her and off to the side. Above her, the bale of straw she crashed into gives way to a pole from which four zip lines are anchored, with three leading up in different directions and one leading to the ground.

The ground cable has a carriage hanging from the top of it, ready to go. Underneath her on the platform, are two more carriages. She pulls herself out of the bale and scans the air with her nose. There's plenty of giant monkey smell, but distant, and there are none to be seen. She drops onto the hill and finds that it is made of stone, which she picks at with her claws to try to determine if it might have been made by the monkeys or is naturally formed.

A great riot of noise below. No longer interested in the origin of the hill, Calypso turns her head and crawls toward the sound. Blurry shapes move on top of two long mounds divided by a valley, but she can't make out what they are. Thundersloth calls threateningly into the valley from the entrance. Then

Calypso thinks she hears Good Boy barking over the hoots and screams of excited giant monkeys. The monkeys quiet down for a moment and she calls to Thundersloth, "*Aaaahhhhiiiieeed!*"

"*Ahhooooooooh!*" Thundersloth responds, looking back over his shoulder.

He heard her! Now she just needs to find a way to get to him.

```
                  /\       /\                        ~ \     / ~
---------------  \ 0     0 /  ------------------    (         )   ----------
                   \   /                             \_/
                    \/
```

The giant sloth drops back to the ground and lumbers down upon Juan Manuel and Good Boy, who run to each side again. The sloth takes a clumsy swing at Juan Manuel, who dodges it with a sideways leap off the wall at the bottom of the stands, launching himself farther down the field. He drags his hooves under bent legs upon landing, barely managing to keep his legs underneath him, before meeting up with Good Boy. The sloth turns to them again.

```
                                    --  -  -
                                 / /        \_
------------------------||||\----¬| /  o  \o |  ----/||||-----------------------
```

The crowd of apes almost hoot in unison, standing in excitement. Her view obstructed by the chimpanzees and her angle to the giant sloth, Shriya stands to see if Good Boy and Juan Manuel made it and Papa puts a hand on her shoulder to make sure she doesn't try to interfere. Over the heads of the chimps, she's relieved to see them jogging to the end of the field.

"Did you see me jump off the side of that wall?" Juan Manuel asks Good Boy.

"No, I missed it when I was trying not to die."

Juan Manuel shakes his head in disappointment. "OK, well, I think I have an idea."

"I'm all ears!"

"That's better than being all nose around this thing!" Juan Manual nods while catching a few breaths. "If we can draw him close enough to the wall, I think I can leap off the side and knock him under the jaw. That might drop him."

Juan Manual takes in the full enormity of the giant sloth coming their way. "But probably not."

"It's better than my plan," Good Boy says. "I got a bite in on him, but he's covered in bone!"

"What do you mean?"

"I mean, his skin has bumps like a turtle shell! If I try to bite into him again, I'll more likely break my teeth."

Juan Manuel's beard shakes. "Well, that's no good, boy."

Good Boy tries to chuckle at the pun, but the sloth is upon them. It stands with its arms spread out, spanning almost the whole width of the field, daring them to pass.

"Go!" Good Boy barks, running across Juan Manuel's side up the middle of the field. Juan Manuel takes the opposite side close to the wall. The sloth swings its arm at Good Boy, knocking him sideways, but missing with its claws.

Juan Manuel makes his leap off the side of the wall with all his power, firing himself at the sloth's head just as it turns toward him. He connects with a terrible crack, knocking the sloth sideways and stumbling toward Good Boy, who scrambles to his feet just in time to avoid getting crushed.

The force of the blow leaves Juan Manuel collapsed on the field in a daze. Good Boy sees him lying helpless and attacks the sloth's exposed leg with extra ferocity. He's able to get his teeth between spots of the skin armor, but the sloth swings at him, forcing him to duck away while the sloth hits his own leg and lets out an angry roar. Good Boy runs past him and tugs at Juan Manuel's horns to rouse him.

"Is he dead?" Juan Manuel asks.

"No," Good Boy barks, "get up!"

"I think *I'm* dead!" Juan Manuel groans.

"Almost! Move!"

Juan Manuel pulls himself up and hops away just as the sloth's claws embed themselves in the ground where he had just been. He and Good Boy get clear and catch their breath at the far end of the field. The crowd celebrates the action.

"I'm so hot right now that I think I could catch fire!" Good Boy pants.

"At least it looks like we dazed it."

"*You* dazed it. Think you can do it again?"

"Maybe," Juan Manual says. "If he'll fall for the same trick, but I'd rather we had another plan."

"One more time and I'll think of something better. Let's test his smarts. Go!" Good Boy runs up the center again. The sloth ignores him and swings around to smash Juan Manuel into the wall. Juan Manuel leaps over the sloth's right arm, slides under its left arm, then hops back onto his hooves to meet up with Good Boy at the far end of the field.

"Did you see that?" Juan Manuel asks with pride.

"Yeah, that was impressive!"

"I don't even know how I did that!"

"How about this?" Good Boy offers, "you go up the middle this time and I'll make it like I'm going up the side. Then you stop in front of him and I cut back and launch off of you and try to take out his eyes."

"Say that again." Juan Manuel asks.

"Go up the middle," Good Boy repeats, trying to be patient. "I'll run to the side, then you stop in front of him, and I'll launch off of you."

"OK, but if I stop, he might squash me!"

"Yes."

"The problem is that I'm trying to *avoid* getting squashed." Juan Manuel screams.

"So, don't let him," Good Boy says. "Now, *go!*"

Juan Manuel takes a deep breath and charges the sloth. The sloth stops and rears up as if to protect its head, with its arms out at each of them. Good Boy cuts back, Juan Manuel turns sideways to a stop, and Good Boy leaps off of his back.

The crowd of chimps goes silent and the world seems to slow. Good Boy has become a harpy eagle, talons extended for the kill as the sloth's head looms in front of him. The wind blowing around his mouth cools him and the sloth's eye is directly in his flight path. The sloth jerks its head away barely enough for Good Boy to miss his eye and land on its shoulder. Fangs biting into flesh, Good Boy is able to spin himself to a halt. With his claws gripping into its fur and the edges of a protective bone patch, Good Boy climbs for its head, but the sloth swings an arm at him and stands to its full height, throwing off Good Boy, who can barely right himself in time to land on his feet. Panting, he limps up to Juan Manuel waiting at the other end of the field.

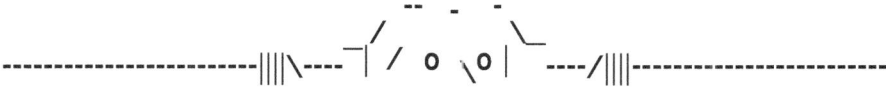

Papa stands to cheer the action with the crowd and, seeing the distraction, Shriya turns to Miguel, "Did you see where they put our guns?"

He looks at her puzzled and points to his ear, "What?"

She yells into his ear, "The guns! Where are they?"

He shrugs and shakes his head, then looks around at the crowd of chimps surrounding them, "Even if we knew, how would we get to them? There are too many monkeys!"

"We could use their heads as stepping stones!" she jokes angrily, but Miguel looks at her blankly. "That old song by The Monkees?" He either doesn't hear her or doesn't get it and she doesn't care. With a huff through clenched teeth to try to calm herself, she turns away from Miguel as Papa sits down beside her and smiles in a way that's nearly human. He signs to her, *dog and goat fight brave.*

Her eyes flash anger at him and she signs, *dog and goat fight for their lives.*

Papa nods in agreement and slaps her lightly on the back.

```
                /\         /\                    ~  \    /  ~
--------------- \ 0      0 / ------------------  ( ‾      ) ‾ ---------
                 \    /                                \ /
                  \  /                                  \_/
                   \/
```

"He's big and dangerous, but he's not a natural fighter." Good Boy says, his tongue hanging out.

"How is that?"

"He divides his focus—he could have killed you or me right there and the one who was left would be an easy win, but he tried to get both of us instead."

"Great," Juan Manuel says, "but I don't see how that's much help here."

"We're still alive, aren't we?"

Juan Manuel just stares at him disapprovingly.

"OK, it was a bad plan, but I can't think very well in this heat."

"Eh, don't feel bad," Juan Manuel says from shaking hooves, "there's only a massive, smelly monster equipped with

90

eagle claws the size of my head pushing us into a wall of big monkeys with sharpened sticks to our backs."

"I have another idea."

"Does it involve surrendering and showering him with compliments?"

"We'll try that if this doesn't work: when he gets here, we lead him back down the field at his fastest pace and into the chimps at the end." Good Boy licks his lips, and shakes off the last of his previous encounter with the sloth. "Run slow enough for him to stay on our tails and we'll cut across each other to the sides at the last moment to avoid the chimps' spears. Maybe the sloth will crash through them and crush them, or they'll get him with their spears."

"Sure," Juan Manuel agrees, breathing hard. "Yeah, OK."

"No smart joke?"

"It's not my last breath yet!"

"I have a feeling it'll be the stink of him that'll take your last breath." Good Boy deadpans.

"Yeah," Juan Manuel agrees with a defiant stomp. "*Why does he smell so bad*?"

"Beats me," Good Boy says. "Calypso doesn't really smell at all. I think the smell is coming from that spot on his stomach. Skunks smell bad, but that's their only defense and they have to spray. This guy . . . he definitely doesn't need anything extra."

The chimps are gathered at the edges of the stands, jumping, howling chaos.

"You know," Juan Manuel observes, "I think these chimpanzees are more like the people than Calypso is like this monster."

"Yeah, you notice the chimpanzees don't have tails like other monkeys do?"

"They don't?" Juan Manuel looks at some of the chimps in the crowd. "Well, what do you know? Maybe they *are* something like people. Explains the bad behavior. Then again, monkeys are also pretty bad."

The giant sloth closes in and Good Boy and Juan Manuel back up as far as they can. "You get ready to run past him on your side, and I'll run past on mine," Good Boy says. "Then stop and we'll pretend we're too tired and hurt to run faster."

"I don't need to pretend." Juan Manuel moans, but taking off as Good Boy barks, "*Go!*"

They both run past the charging sloth, who makes a half swing at Juan Manuel, catching him with a back hand and knocking him farther down the field, skipping and stumbling to stay on his hooves. The sloth lumbers to a stop, then turns and follows. Good Boy and Juan Manuel break into a limping run with Juan Manuel keeping himself just ahead of the galloping beast that's now picking up speed, sensing the end of the fight.

They stay ahead, just out of reach to the end of the field, where the chimps raise their spears at them. At the last moment, they break to the sides of the arena and flatten themselves against the wall. The giant sloth runs by them without even trying to slow down. Two chimps try to raise their spears to the sloth's height, but it barrels through them.

Only one of the spear points cuts the sloth superficially as it glances off a piece of its armored skin and is knocked away. Two guards run for safety and now the crowd erupts in cries of terror. The first two chimps get up and try to grab the control lines to restrain the sloth, but it scoops one of them in a clawed arm and flings him into the stands. The crowd runs and leaps from the wall as another chimp screams through the air into the stands on the other side. The enraged sloth roars at the crowd as two more chimps rush it with raised spears. Standing to his full height, the sloth embraces and smashes the chimps into each other in a crushing bear hug.

"Never accept a hug from a stink sloth!" Juan Manuel jokes, running with Good Boy back to the center of the stands where Shriya, Rondo, and Miguel are dropping onto the field after being abandoned by the panicking chimps. Shriya sees Papa trying to gain control of the crowd, but fear is in command.

The main street entrance to the ball court is blocked by armed chimps trying to contain the giant sloth, so Good Boy, Juan Manuel, Shriya, Miguel, and Rondo all run together toward the back end of the ball court, dodging a screaming chimp that rolls by them in a ball, arms flailing out to the sides trying to stop.

At the back entrance of the ball court, they run into Lindo, who is gathering up his warriors, blocking the most direct way back to the city gate from behind the arena. He sees them and bares his teeth. Good Boy flexes to run at him, but Shriya grabs his collar, nearly having her arm yanked out of her shoulder and getting pulled to the ground, getting her other arm out in time to break her fall. He stops and looks back, whining in concern.

Miguel helps Shriya up and she tugs Good Boy away from Lindo's group. Thundersloth's head looms over the stands and several chimps fly through the air.

They all decide to run for the market street. Lindo glares at them as they join the pressing, pushing chimpanzee jam, and motions for his group to follow him to the fight to get the giant sloth under control.

The energetic furball of flailing creatures meets the friends on the market street, forcing them to go behind the huts in their race toward the pyramid and the gate. A reed hut explodes and burning embers rain down in front of them as the giant sloth trips through the wreckage.

Before the chimps can get over the debris to hold the sloth down, it regains its balance and slams the nearest chimp into the ground, using his crushed body to push itself up to full height. The chimps try to grab the ropes on the sloth, but they're thrown off as the beast spins on its feet, swinging its arms in a circle.

One chimp gets a good grip on a rope and pulls it and another takes a chance on the other rope while the beast is distracted. The sloth grabs the first rope, catches it between two of his massive claws, and yanks it. Having made the mistake of wrapping the rope around his hands for grip, the hapless chimp is now a passenger on Rope Air. He makes a crash landing into the prison hut, collapsing it under his weight. The second chimp screams for help as the sloth jerks its head to him and roars.

A sharp bark from Good Boy gets everyone moving behind him again as he picks his way through the rushing, scrambling simians. He glances back to make sure everyone is following and looks ahead just in time to dodge another chimp. The chimp looks at him with dazed eyes.

As they cross the main street, they encounter several more chimps lying along the road. One sprawls upside down on the stairs of the large pyramid.

Three taught ropes now encircle the sloth, who is beginning to slow from the strain of dragging the chimps around, his head continually reaching back to look at the top of the pyramid. Good Boy notices and follows his gaze, hearing Calypso call out.

"*Aaaahhhhiiiieeee*," she calls.

"Calypso!" Good Boy yells and barks, bringing Juan Manuel to a skidding stop. Rondo and Miguel pass by, but Shriya stops to see where Good Boy is looking.

"It's Calypso!" she yells at the men, pointing to the top of the pyramid where Calypso leans off the zip line pole with her arm outstretched.

Miguel stops, but Rondo continues a few steps before stopping and throwing his arms up in exasperation. "We need to go!"

"Calypso is on top of the pyramid!" Shriya yells.

"How the hell can you even tell?" Rondo yells over the noise. "We need to get out of here while they're distracted!"

Good Boy and Juan Manuel bark and bleat at Shriya. She understands from their looks and ascends the long stairs while they rush the chimps restraining the giant sloth. Miguel grabs a spear off the ground as he runs to follow Shriya.

"Shriya!" Miguel yells and she turns to him, still low enough to catch the spear he tosses to her before pulling out another one from under an injured chimp for himself.

Good Boy launches off the back of one surprised chimp and sinks his teeth into the neck of another holding one of the ropes on the sloth, whipping his body into a spin, and pulling the chimp to the ground while Juan Manuel rushes up the pyramid steps and past Rondo, Miguel, and Shriya to get Calypso.

The exhausted sloth is slowly losing against the army of relentless chimps and Good Boy realizes there's nothing he can do to stop them from restraining the giant beast. Determined to fight to the last with his friends, Good Boy dodges reaching arms and thrusting spear points to rush up the pyramid stairs to help everyone make a final stand, though he hopes the people can think of some way out.

Sensing victory on the ground, some of the chimps notice the people on the pyramid and turn their attention to them, circling around the base. Several race up the two closest stairways. Shriya stabs at the leading chimp with her spear, but the army pushing up behind drives a crowd upwards.

"Get to the top," she tells Rondo and Miguel, "and we'll try to beat them down the other side and make a run for it!"

"The chimps are blocking the road!" Miguel shouts, pointing to the city gate.

"We missed our chance to escape for a damn sloth!" Rondo yells.

"Keep going!" Shriya yells. "We'll try to hold them to a stalemate at the top!" She turns to Rondo. "Maybe they'll take your cowardly ass as a sacrifice."

Before he can respond, a chimp grabs his arm and pulls him in, passing him down the stairs to the bottom. He floats and bobs like he's crowd surfing at a rock show.

"Rondo!" Shriya yells as she and Miguel back their way up the steps.

Good Boy reaches the top to find Calypso settling onto Juan Manuel's back. Shriya and Miguel follow, holding the chimps just out of reach of their spear points on the two occupied stairs.

"We can't cover all four stairs," Miguel says. His shirt is drenched in sweat that relentlessly drips down his face. He wipes it off with a curse.

"Yeah, and the chimps will figure that out soon enough," Shriya says.

"What are chimps?" Calypso asks Juan Manuel.

"Those hairy people—they're called chimpanzees."

"You're making that name up!" Calypso says. "The giant monkeys aren't people!"

"Did you notice they don't have tails? Monkeys have tails. People don't."

"But they're covered in fur," Calypso insists, "and they sometimes walk like monkeys and they climb trees."

Juan Manuel's scan of the four stairs for means of escape comes up short. "You know I love joking around," he says to her and Good Boy, "but the chimps, monkeys, hairy people, whatever are coming up the stairs—*all* of the stairs!"

"Oh, yeah, look at those stairs!" Calypso marvels. "I knew this wasn't just a hill."

Thundersloth is on the ground, restrained by ropes. "*Ahhooooooooh!*" he calls to Calypso.

"*Aaaahhhhiiiieeed!*" she calls back.

"Is Calypso talking to the giant sloth?" Miguel asks in amazement.

Shriya follows Thundersloth's gaze to Calypso, "Yeah," she says, trying to catch her breath, "it sure seems like it."

"What is going on?" Miguel asks in disbelief.

"Hey, I think there's another person!" Calypso calls out to Good Boy, pointing at Rondo. A large chimp is tying him up, not too far from Thundersloth.

"Yeah, he's Shriya's friend that she got caught with," Good Boy answers. "There were other people, too. We already found one of them in the forest."

"Oh, yeah, the dead one against the tree," Calypso says. "Well, the chimpaneezees caught this one again. Whoop, no, look at that! I think he's getting away. Oh, no, now they've got him."

"This doesn't look good," Juan Manuel says as the chimps close in on Rondo from all sides.

Calypso glances at the zip line carriages, but she's pretty sure the carriage can't travel up. Good Boy and Juan Manuel don't have hands to hang on with anyway. The larger blocks of the pyramid between the stairways are arranged like massive steps and are clear of chimps because they're too far apart for the chimps or people to climb. Calypso is sure Juan Manuel and Good Boy could get down them and make a run for it. Not Shriya, though.

"If we can find a way past the chimpaneezees," Calypso says, "we'll have to go right away. We might have to leave that person down there behind."

"We can't," Juan Manuel says. "He's Shriya's friend."

Calypso blinks her version of a shrug. "He's not our friend," she says.

"I'm not sure he's really Shriya's friend," Good Boy growls. "We need to take Shriya with us. The other two? Eh."

Juan Manuel gives them both an angry look. "We all leave, or we all stay!"

"It's a pointless argument, anyway," Good Boy says, looking to the sky.

They hear a zinging, windy sound, and Shriya hits the ground as a chimp from one of the lookout towers passes above her, narrowly missing kicking Shriya in the head. Another thud announces the arrival of the guard from the remaining tower, slamming into the bumper and leaping to his feet. Both guards point short spears at the friends. Good Boy turns to them with a threatening growl and Miguel is able to parry their spears away and push them back to the stairs with the other chimps. It's a small victory.

"Where did they come from?" Good Boy asks, not expecting an answer.

Calypso points to the lookout tower. "They rode down the vines."

He looks at the cables and back at her in amazement. "Is that how you got here?"

"Yes."

"Wasn't there a chimp up there?"

"Yes."

"How did you sneak past it?"

"Oh, he fell down."

"Is that why nothing came down this line?" Juan Manuel asks.

"I came down that line."

"You know what I mean."

"Yes. If I could have gotten to the other chimpaneezee trees first, they wouldn't be here, either." Calypso looks around at the horde of chimps settled on the stairs catching their breaths, content that they have their quarry trapped, and sighs. "I don't think it would have made much difference."

Rondo—his hands tied behind him—is pushed up the stairs that rise along the main street and shoved in front as a shield, forcing Shriya and Miguel to lower their weapons. Good Boy barks at the chimps, but it's all he can do.

With a fearsome shrieking, the king climbs up between the soldiers and howls menacingly, baring his long canine teeth. The soldiers clear space for him and he makes signs to Shriya.

"He's telling us to surrender," Shriya translates. "None of us will be harmed . . . including Buca and Charleston." She points to Calypso and signs to Papa. He looks at her for a moment with puzzled disregard, then nods.

"Calypso, too," Shriya says. The chimp continues to sign.

"He understands that we don't like being in a cage because they were in cages, too, but he cannot let us leave right now," Shriya further translates. "If we continue to help them learn how to live here like humans, he can maintain order. He'll let us go as long as we promise not to bring more men back."

"Of course not," Miguel says. "Tell him we're not like the people who put them in cages. We only want to go back to our lives in peace."

"Tell him that, if he lets us go," Rondo adds, "we can show them how to find clay to make bricks, bowls, and pots."

Miguel adds, "Point out how these animals are our friends, you know, show that we're not the kind of people who would put them in cages."

Shriya and Papa have a sign conversation that ends with Papa nodding and motioning for the soldiers to lower their spears. They all comply, except for Lindo. The rebel chimp steps out from the line near the bottom of the pyramid and rushes up the steps, arms over legs, with a spear in one hand, to face Papa. Papa lifts his spear at him and they hold their weapons on each other like statues. After a moment, Lindo hoots and wails at the rest of the soldiers, who look at one another, raise their spears, and scream and shove as if trying to see who supports who, and which one wants to make the first move to attack. None of them notice the little sloth zipping to the ground on the cable carriage.

Thundersloth sees Calypso crawling slowly toward him and is able to scoot himself closer to her in spite of the ropes binding his arms and legs. She reaches him and pats his chin, then goes to work on the knots of his arms. The giant monkeys don't tie as well as the people, so the first knot is soon loose enough that Thundersloth can pull his arms free. She puts her hand on him to indicate for him to be quiet and moves to his legs.

The noise drops suddenly and Calypso looks up in concern, but Thundersloth has stayed down as if he's still tied. Only the same two giant monkeys with the strange name are yelling and the soldiers have split into two groups, pointing their spears at each other on the stairs. None appear to be looking her way, so she goes back to work on the knots at Thundersloth's feet, holding her breath as much as possible to save herself from his terrible stink.

Once she has freed him, Calypso climbs onto Thundersloth's back, gripping her claws into the fur and marveling at the bony plates she finds. The chimps have split up so that one group surrounds Papa near the top of the pyramid and the other faces them from the bottom. When the chimps near the top see Thundersloth rise quietly to his feet, they start to chatter and scream.

The chimps at the bottom take the warning yells as a threat and several of them panic, stabbing the opposing chimps above them. A new battle erupts. Calypso taps Thundersloth on his shoulder to let him know that it's time. Thundersloth roars and flattens the stakes the human skulls are perched upon at the bottom of the pyramid as he storms onto the steps, tossing chimps like cocoa pods, slashing and smashing with his claws—spears snap, bones crunch, screaming chimps fly through the air or are crushed under his feet, yet she has an easy time holding on from her tall perch between his shoulders. Not such a bad way to travel, she thinks.

The chimps farther up the stairs forget their argument and run in a panic to get over the top of the pyramid and down one of the other sides. The friends and the chimp king crowd against the cushioned zip line anchor pole and are alone when Thundersloth reaches them to stand to his full height and bark his victory, followed by a penetrating growl like nearby thunder. Good Boy steps in front of everyone, barking, growling, fur bristling, lips curled up over his teeth. Juan Manuel steps forward and rises on his back legs with his head lowered. Shriya and Miguel lean into the zipline pole with their spears raised.

Calypso climbs over Thundersloth's shoulder and looks down at them before scratching Thundersloth's head. Good Boy stops barking and looks at her curiously.

"It's Calypso!" Shriya yells with a pointing gesture and she and Miguel lower their spears. Papa looks at the people and decides to do the same, but he and Thundersloth keep their eyes on each other. "How did you get up there?" Shriya asks.

Calypso turns her head toward the zip line and the people look at each other in shock. "Can she understand you?" Miguel asks, cutting Rondo's restraints.

"She's likely looking at the trees," Rondo says. "She probably wants to go back to them and I'd gladly go with her."

"Or she's telling us she traveled down the zip line," Shriya counters.

"I can admit she's clever, but come on!—she's still just a sloth."

"This is my friend, Thundersloth," Calypso says to Good Boy and Juan Manuel.

"That's a good name," Juan Manuel says.

"How did you know he's a sloth?" Good Boy asks.

"Look at his claws! He walks on the sides of his feet, and his call is like a big version of mine."

"The people said he's a sloth, too," Good Boy says. "Some kind of a stink sloth. I thought he was a bear."

"*Stinksloth* is an even better name," Juan Manuel nods.

Thundersloth's low growl vibrates everyone's chests.

"OK, we'll stick with Thundersloth!" Juan Manuel says, but Thundersloth turns around and roars at some chimps sneaking up behind him. The chimps shrink back and return to the ground to help the rest of them get the wounded and dead away from the pyramid.

Calypso climbs down Thundersloth's arm and onto Good Boy's back.

"Yikes, you stink like him, now!" Good Boy complains.

"Now you know what it was like for me and your farts!"

"My farts are never this bad!"

"Says you," Juan Manuel interjects.

Thundersloth swipes at a lone chimp coming up from one of the side stairs and it also loses courage.

"OK, so you're fine with this monster being a sloth, but you choose to call the other sloths that live in the trees *tree bears* instead?" Juan Manuel asks.

Calypso nods from her perch on Good Boy's back.

"That makes no sense."

"Yes, it does."

Papa pulls on Shriya's shirt to get her attention and signs to her. She signs back to him and they have a short conversation.

"What did he say?" Miguel asks.

"He asked what kind of animal Calypso is, so I told him she's a small sloth—a slow animal that lives in the trees," Shriya tells him. "He asked what she's wearing on her head, so I told him they're glasses that keep the bright sun from hurting her eyes. He asked if she made them and I told him that people made them for her."

"Maybe you should have let him think she made them herself so he might be more afraid," Miguel says.

Shriya smiles at Calypso. "I think she's proven capable enough on her own."

The king gets her attention again and they have another conversation. "He's asking how Calypso controls the giant sloth—though, he called it a bear—and I'm telling him that it's probably because they're both different kinds of sloths even though that's obviously a nonsense explanation." Shriya laughs. "He says that's impressive because he can't even control his own kind. I told him that this sloth is very special—not like normal tree sloths."

"He thought the giant sloth was a bear? Not a bad guess," Rondo shrugs.

"Am I the only one who doesn't know what a bear is?" Juan Manuel asks Good Boy.

"Tell him we're all leaving now and the giant sloth is going to lead us out whether he likes it or not," Rondo suggests.

"I can tell him that," Shriya says, "but how are you going to tell Calypso so she can get him to do it?"

"Calypso drives a boat and rides other animals like horses," Miguel laughs, "she's probably way ahead of us!"

Thundersloth climbs toward one of the other stairways and takes a swipe at another chimp.

"We can't stay here forever, so what do you think we should do?" Rondo asks, and Shriya signs it to Papa.

Papa signs that he wants to let them all leave. Shriya responds that the giant sloth is to be set free, too, but Papa shakes his head. His hands rapidly sign and Shriya translates again.

"He can't let us go now, but he can help us escape later," Shriya tells them. "The giant sloth has to stay. They need him and if he lets him go free, the chimps will revolt. Also, his cave is just outside the city, so it's not like there's anywhere for him to go."

Papa signs again and the two have another short conversation.

"He says we must go with him back to the cage," Shriya says. "I told him it was destroyed and he said he has another option that will be nicer."

Shriya signs that they will surrender and Papa climbs to the top of the pole so everyone can see him behind Thundersloth. He waves his arms and shouts to get the attention of the rest of the chimps, then declares his decision to the masses. Lindo stands at the foot of the stairs behind them and many of the remaining chimps gather to his side. Everyone turns to face the crowd and Thundersloth barks a warning over their shoulders. Papa and Lindo alternate between signing and screaming at each other, and Shriya interprets the argument for everyone.

"Lindo says that we can't be allowed to leave because we will return with more men and hurt them again." She shakes her head. "Damn people! I can't blame the chimps for hating us. Who knows what's been done to them? They probably assume they'll be sent back to the lab."

Papa looks down on them. Shriya signs emphatically that they will not bring anyone back, that this place has been a secret from man for hundreds of years and can remain a secret. Papa relays this to the crowd, but Lindo angrily replies that men lie. Shriya signs that she is a woman, but the chimps aren't convinced there's enough of a difference. Lindo demands that the people will either stay to help them build the city or be killed.

Calypso slowly waves the claws and the wrist of one arm around in mocking imitation, and taps Good Boy. "What are they doing?" she asks.

"It's some kind of way of talking."

"Do you mean to tell me that monkeys can talk this quiet way? Why are they always so loud?" She blinks her eyes and shakes her head disapprovingly. "And why can Shriya speak monkey?"

"I don't know," Good Boy says.

"I think maybe you were right," Juan Manuel joins in. "These aren't giant monkeys, they're a type of people."

"So, they want to keep the people here?" Calypso asks.

"Sounds like it," Good Boy says. "They think if they let them go, they'll bring more people back and hurt them."

Calypso gives a slow blink. "That fear makes sense, but then they'll . . . wait, I missed it! What did Shriya just say? What's a lab?"

"A kind of dog, isn't it?" Juan Manuel answers.

Good Boy nods. "It is, but I don't think that's what they're talking about."

"Shriya said the monkeys think they'll be sent back to a lab . . . do you think that means the people will turn them back into dogs?" Juan Manuel asks. "Can they do that?"

"I don't think . . . well, they can fly, so . . . maybe?"

"Then *we* can probably leave," Calypso suggests.

"I'm not leaving Shriya," Good Boy says.

"Not forever!" Calypso says. "Just for a little while so we can come back with a bunch more people and they can turn these giant monkeys back into dogs. How do you think they do that?"

"I have no idea," Good Boy says, "but I don't know how they do most things."

"Do you think it hurts?" Juan Manuel asks.

Good Boy looks at Juan Manuel. "It must, right? It would certainly feel weird, at least."

"Hurts or not," Juan Manuel says, "I wouldn't want to be a dog."

"Why not?" Good Boy asks. "People wouldn't be trying to eat you. And you could fight better."

"I think I can fight just fine. dog," Juan Manuel sneers.

"For a goat. Now just imagine if you had claws and sharp teeth!"

"Yeah, that would be better in a fight, but I need to keep the horns."

"Why?"

"I like the horns!"

Calypso looks at the both of them. "I don't think the people can turn one creature into another," she says. "They must be talking about something else. Maybe a lab is a place. Where did they even come from, monkeys this big? Do you think they come from a pace with even bigger trees?"

"What if they can, though?" Juan Manuel asks with worry.

"Then you can't keep your horns!" Calypso says with exasperation.

"How do *you* know?"

"Because then you wouldn't be a dog or a goat, you'd be dog-goat," she says. "A *doat*. Do you want to be a doat?"

"I don't know. Maybe."

She pushes on his horn playfully. "We need to think up a plan. My idea is to get the giant monkeys to let us go so we can get back to the boat and get some more people. What do you two have?"

"Nothing," Good Boy admits, "but how are we going to get more people to come back with us?"

"Do you know more good people?" Calypso asks him.

"Not that I can get to understand us enough to follow us back here," he says, pointing his nose. "Miguel was the best we could get, and he came on his own. Our options only get worse."

"I don't think he's dumb," Juan Manuel says.

"He's dumb for a person."

"He's not as smart as Shriya," Juan Miguel agrees, "but the reason you don't like him is because you're jealous."

"You keep saying that, but it doesn't make it true."

Calypso sighs. "Forget it. I'll climb onto Thundersloth and get him to just squash all the monkeys."

"There's too many—they'll stop him again." Juan Manuel says.

She scratches her head and thinks for a few moments while Papa and Lindo continue to argue and Shriya tries to follow and translate for Miguel and Rondo. "They can only stop him if they work together, and look at them—they're about to fight each other. If we can get them to fight, we can escape. Maybe we all can escape."

"Why are we in a place where a sloth is planning our battle?" Juan Manuel asks.

Papa's screams interrupt them. His propeller spinner crown pings down the pyramid steps, and a small band of Lindo's soldiers sneak up behind them all and poke them with the points of their spears, disarming the people and Papa's most loyal soldiers.

They're surrounded. Thundersloth rumbles at the rabble ascending the stairs, but one of the chimps sneaks onto his back, grabs his control lines, and jabs him in the neck with a sharpened stick.

"Well, this isn't good," Good Boy says between barking threats to the chimps. "I guess they didn't need that many to stop him after all."

"How did they sneak up on us?" Juan Manuel asks, looking at Good Boy.

Good Boy growls. "How can I smell anything with that stink sloth in my nose!"

"Maybe if the two fast, fighting animals had a plan instead of leaving the sloth to come up with it, they wouldn't have had time to sneak up behind us!" Calypso scolds them.

"Can't argue with that," Good Boy says before barking at the chimp aiming a spear point at him.

"If they can turn dogs into giant monkeys and back, do you think they can turn you into a monkey?" Juan Manuel asks Good Boy.

"This is what you're asking me right now?"

"I'd just like to know before we die."

Their chimp captors lead everyone, including Papa, down the stairs and around the back of the pyramid where they are pushed through an open doorway. A whip cracks and a protesting Thundersloth reluctantly rolls a giant stone ball across the doorway to block their escape. The chimps stuff the open space around it with soil and stones. Papa stares out a larger hole and Lindo stares at him from the outside. They sign briefly to each other before Lindo laughs silently and steps aside for some of the other chimps to stuff the hole shut. The friends inspect the layout of the chamber and, a short while later, the human and chimp eyes adjust to the dark enough to see its outline in the fast disappearing light that still sneaks past the ball.

Rondo examines the stone, running his hands along its smooth face as the chimps finish stuffing dirt around it from outside. "Does it make anyone feel better to know that sphere is probably a Diquís stone? That's probably the biggest one ever found."

"A fascinating archaeological curiosity," Shriya says. "When this place is rediscovered, we'll be archaeological curiosities, too. Can you imagine what they'll wonder when they find the bones of three people, a chimpanzee, a dog, a goat, a sloth, and some cell phones from a thousand years after this place was originally abandoned?"

"I guarantee their guesses will be way off," Rondo says.

"You think people will still be around by then?" Miguel asks.

"Maybe they'll be chimpanzee archaeologists," Rondo suggests.

"Or sloths," Shriya adds.

"Or sloths," Miguel agrees. "Rondo, would there be another way out of here? I don't know what monkey business they have planned for us, but I'd rather not wait."

"Since this is likely a burial chamber, there probably isn't," Ronda says with a sigh. "At least not in the physical sense."

"Well, that's convenient," Shriya says, looking at the last shaft of light streaming in.

Papa screams at the traitorous chimps, but it has no effect.

With the doorway completely blocked, Miguel turns on his phone light and shines it around. Statues of Mayan gods stare at them from the sides of the chamber, but they're of no help getting out.

The statues seem to dance in the movement of light and shadow. Calypso touches one of them to feel that they're stone, just to make sure. The place smells funny and she wishes she was up in the trees.

Shriya signs to Papa, but he shakes his head. Papa signs something to her and points to the statue against the closest wall.

"Lindo thinks we're too dangerous and Papa is too trusting of people," she translates. "Papa asked for a fight between himself and Lindo to settle it. Lindo didn't respond either way, but Papa thinks Lindo might come back after we haven't eaten for a couple days to fight to legitimize his rule."

Papa signs again.

"Now he's asking what the statues are."

"Tell him that people made them," Rondo says. "We believe they are representations of gods, and implore them to

108

look after the dead ancient kings who were buried here. Tell him this was a great culture of ancient people."

"I don't know how I'm going to explain all that," Shriya says with a sigh, signing back and forth with Papa for a bit. " He asked what happened to the people here and I told him that many strong people on boats from far away came with guns and defeated the people. He doesn't like that, doesn't like peoples' guns, but he says you're wrong about this being a burial chamber."

"Oh," Rondo scoffs, "the chimp knows better than the archaeologist!"

"We should probably be looking for a way out before my battery dies instead of giving history lessons and arguing about theories," Miguel says, turning his light around the chamber.

"No, wait!" Shriya grabs Miguel's wrist and turns the light back to Papa, who signs something to her. "He says this isn't a burial chamber because there are no bones in it, but that there is a connected tunnel that has many bones."

"Is it an exit?" Miguel asks.

Shriya signs the question to Papa. He shakes his head and shrugs, then signs something back.

"He doesn't know, but there's a cave entrance at the back of the room."

"A cave?"

"I think he means a doorway."

"Well, have him lead the way!" Miguel gives Papa room to move and walks behind him with the light over his shoulder. The rest follow behind.

An archway guarded on each side by stylized stone jaguars is filled in with large blocks except for a small space by the top. After a little clearing of accumulated dirt and pushing one of the smaller loose blocks, everyone squeezes through the hole except for Juan Manuel, who can't get in past his front legs. He bleats in desperation and Good Boy tries digging the hole larger, but the stones are too big and heavy. Though Miguel and

Rondo are able to remove a few more small ones, they can't dislodge any of the large blocks, which isn't quite enough for Juan Manuel to fit through.

"Can you get sideways?" Good Boy asks.

"No, it's too high off the ground!"

Miguel kicks over the stone they dislodged and uses it to leverage himself against the highest stone in the doorway, but it rolls away instead of holding him. He exhales and shakes his head. "We need something heavier behind us."

"Yeah, all we need to do is pull one of the really big ones out and use that as a brace," Rondo says sarcastically.

"If we could pull one out, we wouldn't need to push the rest," Miguel insists.

"Yeah, that's the joke."

"At least I'm trying to help!" Miguel says, his temper flaring. "What are you doing, besides explaining human murder history to chimpanzees?"

"Both of you stop," Shriya admonishes. "Let's see if this is even a way out."

Juan Manuel sticks his head through the hole and bleats to everyone for the last time.

"This probably isn't a way out, and we'll be coming back soon," Good Boy assures him. "And if it is a way out, we'll be coming back to get you."

Juan Manuel sadly nods his head, hoping the dim light can hide the fear in his eyes. "It's OK. Get out and get away."

"We won't leave without coming back for you," Good Boy asserts.

"I don't want anyone dying for me! Just go." With that, Juan Manuel goes to pull his head back inside, but his horns catch, so he curses and adjusts the angle of his head before trying again and disappearing back into the first chamber.

Shriya wipes her eyes and Miguel swallows hard—all the humans saw was a dog and a goat appearing to have some silent correspondence, but they somehow know what was said. Papa tugs on Miguel's shirt. He looks down and clears his throat, "We need to go."

Ahead of the cone of light thrown by the phone, the tunnel walls glitter and shine like stars, reminding Calypso of her climb through the sacred tree on the small land of the weird sheep.

Rondo nearly trips on the uneven ground in the dim light.

"What's that shining on the walls?" Miguel asks.

"Pyrite. Fool's gold." Rondo crouches down and moves his hands around his feet for something. "In Mayan cities—if that's what this is—it is believed that the temples represent the emergence of life in the solar system. There are temples for the moon and the sun with the land of the dead in between. The Mayan placed the minerals into the walls to represent the stars." He holds up part of an adult human femur. "Would you look at that! Perfect timing, huh?"

"Yeah. It makes me feel real reassured about our chances of getting out," Miguel complains.

"It was likely a high honor to be buried here."

"You're welcome to stay."

They continue descending the tunnel until it ends in flood water.

"Well, who's up for a swim?" Shriya asks.

Rondo asks Miguel to shine the light behind them and nods. "I don't know why this tunnel descends, but it's pretty straight. Which way would you say this tunnel is leading, guessing by where we entered it under the pyramid?"

"I don't know," Miguel shrugs, "maybe the smaller pyramid?"

"Shriya?" Rondo asks.

"Yeah, I'd say the same."

"Then we all agree," Rondo says. "If that's where it leads—and it makes sense that it would—I'd say we've walked probably two thirds of the way there. It might be only about another thirty meters to the pyramid."

"Only? Do you think we're seriously going to swim that?" Miguel asks. "We don't even know where it really leads! If it's blocked off at the other end, I don't think we'd be able to make it back. Are any of us pearl divers?"

Noisy giants! Calypso thinks, shaking her head. "What are they getting on about?" she asks Good Boy.

"The passage is blocked by water," he explains.

"Yes."

"They're arguing about how they could swim it."

"Arguing why?" Calypso asks. "Just swim it."

"It's far, and they don't think they'll have enough air to swim underwater."

"How far is it?"

"I don't know, but it sounds like they think it's less than we just walked."

Calypso turns her head to look behind her. "I can swim that."

"But we don't know how long it actually is," Good Boy says.

"Swimming it will tell us."

"What if there's a monster in there?"

"Then it will eat me," Calypso says, resigned, "and you'll know that's not a way out."

"What if it's blocked?" Good Boy asks.

"Then I'll swim back."

"What if it's too far?"

"Sloths can hold our breath a long time."

"You need to because you're so slow."

She pauses for a moment to let that joke hit the floor and die so it can decay with the human bones. "If I haven't made it to the end by the time I think I still have enough breath to return, I'll swim back."

"That sounds dangerous."

"So is staying here."

"I know you can do a lot for a sloth," Good Boy says, "but even if you make it, we won't be able to go with you."

"OK."

Good Boy cocks his head at her. "OK?"

"I'll get Thundersloth and have him move that stone."

"How will you get him away from the chimpanzees?"

"I'll get him at night," Calypso says. "He goes to his cave to sleep."

"How are you going to get there?"

"Same way I got here."

"But the towers have guards up there all night."

Calypso waves off that thought. "Don't worry about them."

"Don't worry?"

"Yeah, you worry too much." Calypso climbs off Good Boy's back and crawls to the water. Good Boy barks at Miguel, who almost steps on Calypso by mistake. She looks up at him then keeps going. Once she reaches the water, Shriya runs over and picks her up .

"Whoa, where are you going?" Shriya asks. "You'll drown in there, Calypso!"

Calypso turns her head and reaches for the water, but Shriya doesn't seem to notice. Calypso looks at Good Boy and gives her blink-stare version of a shrug. He barks at Shriya, a hollow echo in the tunnel.

"Quiet, you," Shriya commands. "Calypso can't swim this, it's probably too far even for us." She puts Calypso back on top of Good Boy and turns to the others. "We might as well go back and make Charleston feel better."

The people and Papa walk past Good Boy and Calypso, who follow them back. "Are you sure you can swim that?" Good Boy asks.

"Yes." She's just not sure she'll make it back out.

"Then I'll sneak you back when they're sleeping."

"But, they sleep when the sky fire goes out! If I miss the changing of the tree guard, I'll have to wait until the morning one comes down so I can catch a ride up. If that happens, I won't be able to get Thundersloth back here until tomorrow night."

"What do you mean, a ride up?"

"A ride on the vine that the chimpaneezees use to get off the towers."

"How will you go up it?"

"I think if I grab the stick that rides it . . ." Calypso stops and scratches her head. "Oh. You're right—that won't work. The giant monkey people climb up the towers carrying the stick things with them, they don't ride up. It would be a long way to Thundersloth's den, even if I could get up there. I'll have to find him in the day and figure something out."

"I'll go with you."

"You can't hold your breath that long," she says, and they both go quiet.

Good Boy finally breaks the long silence. "Well, it sounds like we're going to be hungry."

"There will be plenty of giant monkeys to eat when I get back with Thundersloth," Calypso says.

"From what I can tell, they don't taste good," Good Boy tells her, "but I'll probably be too hungry to care."

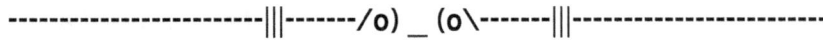

"Are you sure about this?" Good Boy asks as Calypso slips off his back onto the tunnel floor.

"Who else can do it?" she asks.

"The people have a plan."

"Yes, to jump the giant monkeys when they come in," Calypso says. "I don't see why that would work this time when it didn't work before."

Good Boy scratches behind his ear and wonders if the monkeys have fleas that aren't bothered by his flea collar. "Because the monkeys will have a narrow opening so that only one or two can get inside at a time and they won't be able to get behind us or from the sides."

"I can't help with that, so while you fight, I'll do this. If their plan works out, then you can find *me*." She crawls toward the water.

"Calypso!" Good Boy barks.

She stops.

"I wish I could come with you," he says heavily.

"Even if you could hold your breath long enough, you're better off here."

"That's not what I mean."

"I know." She passes him her sunglasses and slips into the cold water, immediately questioning her decision. Soon reaching the submerged part of the tunnel, she takes a deep breath and feels her way forward with her forehead and claws, her natural buoyancy keeping her at the top of the tunnel.

Good Boy whines, then swallows his worry and returns to the chamber to try to get some sleep before the chimps come for them.

The cold of the water has cut deep into Calypso's bones, slowing her movements, and her head is sore from rubbing and bouncing along the roof of the tunnel. After a long time of getting bumped in the same place, she shifts her head down, but all that does is expand the area of soreness. It's quite possible that the tunnel has no end, she thinks, or maybe there's just no end of it for her. A little bit farther, a little bit more, one claw in front of the other until she reaches whatever end awaits.

*Skritch!* Her claws stop on a blockage and she freezes in panic that it may be a dead end. She's used so much energy getting here that she's not sure she has the air and body heat to get back. After a moment, Calypso forces her brain to work again and feels around from the wall on one side and across to the other for an opening. It seems that the tunnel is sealed.

If she turns around now, there's a slight chance she might just be able to make it back, but for what? It's likely that the chimpanzees will just kill them all. *No!* The claws on her hands and feet dig into the sides of the wall to force herself down against her buoyancy, biting into the tunnel and the blockage with every claw she has. A reach and a miss where there must be a hole and her other claw slips. Calypso's whole body floats back to the top, the bump forcing out some precious air.

Lungs burning and body freezing, she tries again, making it down to where the pressure felt about the same as when she slipped, and she more carefully reaches out. Nothing—*nothing!* Getting a good bite with her hands, Calypso lets go with her feet and hangs upside down on the edge of a hole. Reaching into the void and swallowing her fear, she pulls herself in.

She half swims and half crawls upside down now, finding she can propel herself off the ceiling with her claws to make faster progress. The water pressure lessens, but her lungs sear in pain, her muscles ache from the cold, and she is having trouble thinking. Pulling herself along, her body begins to get strangely warm, her worries melt away, and she sees a light ahead with something fuzzy in it. A sloth hand reaches out of the light for her and her mother's face comes into focus. A sense of peacefulness travels like a warm wave through her and she stops crawling, yet her body keeps moving forward, bouncing gently along the roof of the tunnel, the light . . .

```
                   / \     / \          ~  \     /  ~
----------------  \ 0    0 / ----------------  (        )  ----------
                   \   /                            \ /
                    \ /                              \_/
```

. . . the light gets brighter.

Beams of morning sunlight shine through the breaks in the doorway as the chimp soldiers clear away debris, and Papa hoots quietly to get everyone's attention. Papa, Rondo, Miguel, and Shriya stand to either side of the doorway, as hidden as they can be by the walls to its sides. They hold clubs made of leg bones from the long deceased inhabitants of the city.

Good Boy and Juan Manuel stand side by side in the dark, ready to charge as soon as the chimp soldiers enter. This is a good plan, Good Boy nods to himself. If the people can get the spears off the first soldiers who enter, they might be able to fight off enough of them the king chimp to regain his place at the top of the pack with this show of power. Maybe. More debris is cleared away and the smell of the giant sloth enters the chamber. Good Boy feels a pit of worry about Calypso in his stomach, but he tells himself that she wouldn't have had time to get to the giant sloth even if she made it through the tunnel.

"Thundersloth is out there helping the chimps," Juan Manuel says with worry and a hint of blame.

" Calypso couldn't have made it to him," Good Boy says. "She could be waiting for a chance to call out to him."

"If she made it out."

"I know, goat!"

"Or maybe they captured her."

"Who do you want to fight," Good Boy growls, "me, or the chimpanzees?"

Juan Manuel shakes his head and aims his horns at the chamber entrance. "I'll see how it goes with the chimpanzees first."

Thundersloth grunts with effort, his huge arms wrapped around the stone sphere, his claws digging into the rock. With a shower of small stones and dirt, the ball begins to roll away. A billowing cloud of falling dust partly obscures the expanding daylight like campfire smoke as he pulls the ball from the doorway.

As the stone clears the entrance, two chimp soldiers rush in with their spears leveled in front of them. Papa jumps up and blows dirt into their eyes. Shriya, Miguel, and Rondo step out from the shadows and break the bone clubs over the chimp soldier's heads, grabbing their spears from them and immediately turning just in time to use them on the next set of chimps that try to enter.

The deafening shock of the screams echoing in the chamber and the stench of Thundersloth assaults their ears and nostrils as another pair of chimps leap over their fallen comrades. Shriya, Miguel, and Rondo try to remove the spears from the dead chimps to train them on the reinforcements. The chimps are too fast, so Good Boy and Juan Manuel charge them with slashing teeth and horns. One of the soldiers tries to shake Good Boy off, but his teeth are locked into the chimp's shoulder.

The second chimp grabs Juan Manuel by the horns and tries to twist his neck—*crack*! The soldier drops and Papa lifts a black stone statue out of his skull to swing at another traitor. With Shriya's spear now free and Miguel having grabbed a different one off the chimp taken out by Papa, all three of the people ready their weapons for the next set of soldiers.

The first chimp that had come through the door gets back and lands a blow on Rondo that knocks him against the wall and to the floor. Papa swings the statue at a chimp fighting Good Boy, knocking him down into the darkness alongside the doorway, then finishing him off with a blow to the head. Shriya and Miguel push against the broken shaft of a spear that's stuck in the side of another chimp holding him in the doorway and blocking more of them from coming in.

Papa picks up another discarded spear and stabs the stuck soldier through the neck. A new chimp immediately makes his way through the doorway over the body and Good Boy grabs the shaft of his spear with his teeth, holding him for Juan Manuel to catch him under the chin with a terrible sideways uppercut. The crack and pop echo over the din of combat and the bodies are now piled up in the doorway, preventing more from easily entering.

Additional soldiers reach as close as they dare to pull their fallen out of the way, giving the defenders some time to catch their breath. As the dead and injured chimps are dragged off the top of the heap, Shriya and Miguel rush outside, using their stolen spears to add the two closest chimps to the pile. They withdraw back to the tomb and with a shrieking war cry, Papa pushes between them and leaps over the bloody mess, landing with a heavy stomp on the torn up grass outside, clearing a circle within the dwindling number of brave soldiers with a whipping spear point and bared fangs. Miguel and Shriya scramble out behind him. Good Boy barks a warning about the risky change in strategy, then follows, putting his back to the wall of the pyramid with every tooth he owns on display.

Juan Manuel hops out and spots an ambush on the wall. "Behind us!" he bleats.

Shriya and Miguel hear the goat alarm and raise their spears just in time to dissuade three chimp soldiers from leaping on their backs.

The crowd surrounding Papa parts and Lindo enters the circle wearing the scratched, dented crown and wielding a spear. The soldiers on the pyramid jump down and gather around the circle in two separate groups on opposing sides. They all start to hoot and scream and bang the butts of their spears against the ground.

The king knocks off Lindo's crown with a precise poke from the point of his spear and the crowd goes still. The quiet lasts but a few moments before it is broken by a roar from Thundersloth. Two of his handlers with several guards for backup lead him out to the jungle's edge and tie him to a tree before hurrying back to watch the fight for the future of the ape city.

Stale air smelling of musty soil and fetid water is the most welcome scent Calypso has ever experienced. She drags herself out of the flooded tunnel, through a large hole in a walled up tunnel doorway, and onto the floor of a stone chamber dripping filth that forms a puddle. The light is gone, leaving complete darkness behind, but it's a little bit warmer and she needs that after the cold tunnel has sapped her energy.

If only there was something to eat! Her nose can find no trace of edible vegetation in the air. After resting for a little while to regain her strength, Calypso turns to the side and bumps into a wall that she decides to follow in hope of finding an exit. She soon finds things piled in her way that feel like they may be cut up branches held together by stiff moss. They don't smell or feel edible, so she tries to climb over them, pulling a heap of sticks down upon her. Something particularly heavy rolls over her back and clops and clangs onto the floor in a racket that freezes her for a few moments.

She listens for any predators. Nothing but a drip of water from her runoff. Satisfied enough that it's safe to continue, Calypso clumsily pulls her way through and over the unstable mound to find the wall again, disappointed to not find a tree. Pushing on, she finds another bound up pile that collapses as she climbs over it. The third pile is flatter, and easier to climb over, but she's very tired and starting to worry that she's not going to find a way out other than going back through the tunnel, which she lacks the energy for.

A draft rustles Calypso's fur. She turns her head to face the source of the air and crawls toward it. Something like a snake brushes her face and she freezes—not breathing, heart not beating—hoping it thinks she's part of the piles of sticks. It brushes her face again, this time holding itself there. She's been discovered!

As a last defense, she swipes at it, her claw catching stiff, woody material. It's not a snake after all. Pulling it to her, she hooks her claw into the hanging thing that feels like a vine—old and dried, but she knows it must lead somewhere out of this place. Calypso reaches up and carefully pulls her weight onto the vine. It seems strong enough to hold, so she climbs up to the source of the falling air.

She's exhausted and goes extra slowly, but eventually Calypso reaches a stone ledge off of which the vine has draped itself. Gripping with her legs to reach as far as she can with her arms, she's able to drag herself onto the top of the ledge, finding herself on what feels like another stone floor covered in a thin layer of dirt. It's a bit warmer in the new room, though she's still uncomfortably cold.

Stopping to rest and cast her nose around to smell a possible exit, Calypso eyes pick up a sharp pin of light hitting the edge of a doorway across from her. Even though the light isn't enough to meaningfully illuminate the place, it tells her there's a way out, and that the sky fire must be burning outside. It's too late to catch Thundersloth alone. Either way, Calypso needs to get out, so she heads toward the light with as much energy as she can muster. The dirt on the floor clings to her drying fur as she pulls herself along and all she wants to do is rest, but she needs to get warm and find Thundersloth to help her friends, so she doesn't have any more time for that.

Vibrations in the ground! Stopping in panic, Calypso hears only silence, heavy and stifling—nothing but her heartbeat. She waits a moment, then drags herself forward a little more and stops to see if the vibrations return. Nothing, but she can't shake the feeling that she's not alone. Moving on, this time she's sure that something scampers along the floor ahead of her, and she stops again. It's too dark to see much more than the outline of the doorway and walls alongside it, so she listens, smells, and feels for vibrations. Whatever it is has patience.

Urine! But the smell is from an unknown creature, if not completely unfamiliar. Something is in here, and Calypso doesn't want to know what it is. As she continues moving cautiously along, the sound of her claws scraping at the floor and her fur dragging along the dirt and dust seem so loud that she might as well be a tree full of drunk monkeys. The feeling of vulnerability is overwhelming, pounding in her head, driving her on, one limb outstretched, then another, ever closer to the source of the light.

Something flutters past Calypso with furious speed, kicking up dust in its wake that makes her sneeze. It races around to her other side and she swipes at it, but she's far too slow. By the breeze of its wake, she can tell that whatever else is here is smaller than her, but that calms her only slightly, as it's also very fast. There's an aggressive thump in the darkness beyond the outline of the doorway.

"How did you get in here?" something asks in Common language, forcefully projecting the words into her mind to appear more intimidating than it is.

"I swam." She responds.

"You swam?" the voice challenges. "There's no water in here! Where did you make your hole to break into our burrow?"

"I told you that I swam," Calypso says. "There's water in the hole behind me."

"There is not," the voice says defiantly.

"Of course there is! That's how I got here," Calypso says. "If you live here, how would you not know there's water down there?"

"I've never been down there," the voice concedes, no longer pushing its words with greater force.

"Then why are you telling me like you know better?" she asks in annoyance, no longer afraid.

After a moment, the voice continues, "Maybe there *is* water down there, then what are you?"

"I'm a tree-hanger, but the people call us sloths."

"What do you eat?"

"I live in trees and eat leaves," Calypso says.

"Trees? What are you doing here?"

She's losing patience with this voice, but she doesn't want to get it angry. "I'm trying to get outside," she says. "I was trapped on the other side of the tunnel of water, so I came here looking for a way out. It looks like there's one ahead."

"There is," the voice admits, "but the burrow entrance is too small for you."

"I don't think this is a burrow," Calypso counters. "From what I could understand the people say, this was built by people many, many sky fires before we were even alive."

"What are people?" the voice asks.

"Noisy giants."

"I don't know what they are."

122

"They're the tall creatures outside of this place that walk on their back legs, but they don't have fur like the chimpa . . . chimpey . . ." Calypso blinks in the dim light. "I forget what the people call them, but they're the giant monkey things out there. People are like them without fur."

The creature pauses for a moment. "Yes, I know what you mean now—the giant monkeys are noisy and they eat us. We call them aahks-hoots. They're terrible."

Calypso relaxes a little more knowing that whatever it is she's talking to can't be very dangerous if they're eaten by the giant monkeys. "I prefer it quiet, too."

"It is told that, for generations, we had quiet, until those aahks-hoots came from the sky and occupied this territory." The voice sounds sad, and irritated. Calypso thinks she would be upset, too, if she lost all her quiet.

"The giant monkeys don't fly," she says. "They ride down from the trees on vines. I did the same thing to get from the trees to the other stone hill the people made."

"The aahks-hoots themselves don't fly, they were brought here. My ancestors told us that they came here in the talons of two great eagles. The eagles were greedy and caught more aahks-hoos than they could carry, so many that the weight of all of them was too great for the eagles. They crashed and died, and the aahks-hoots tore the eagles apart and ate them."

Calypso is fascinated, but also still needs to get moving. "I don't know about all that. I just came here to help my friends who were taken by the aksoos," she says.

"Aahks-hoots. Those are the sounds they make."

"So, what are you?" Calypso asks.

"We're the shtishtish."

"I don't know what that is."

The creature walks carefully into the light from the door frame and stands up for it to illuminate him.

"Oh, I know what you are!" Calypso says. "The people call you rabbits. You eat the ground leaves. There were rabbits where I lived with the Man. They'd always run away before I got a good look at them, but I know you by the ears. You're very quiet. I like rabbits. How do you speak the common language?"

The rabbit steps back into the comfort of the darkness. "We learned it from the goats and the donkeys. We like to eat with them because the kill birds stay away. How did you learn it in the trees?"

"My dog friend taught me when I lived with a person," Calypso tells the rabbit.

The rabbit steps a little closer. "Why did you live with a person?"

"He was a nice person who saved me after my mother was killed."

"That does sound nice."

"Some of them are," Calypso says slowly. "But some of them are terrible. They even kill each other. That good person was killed by other people."

The rabbit folds his ears back. "Did they eat him?"

"No. I don't think they eat each other."

"Then why did they do that," the rabbit asks.

"I don't know. He was nice."

"The aahks-hoots eat us," the rabbit says. "We are safe from them in here, but you say the people built this place? How did they do that?"

"I don't know," Calypso says. "I've been told that they made everything but the ground, the trees, and us."

"Who told you that?" the rabbit asks.

"Good Boy, my dog friend."

"What is a dog? They sound wise."

"Sometimes," Calypso says. "He's taller than me, walks on four legs, has a long nose with big teeth. Some dogs are really small. They're all noisy, though."

"I think I know the creature you mean. They eat us, too." The rabbit takes a wary step back. "How can you be friends with one?"

"He lived with me and the man."

The rabbit is quiet for a few moments, so Calypso starts crawling again.

"Where's the hole you made?" The rabbit squeaks. "That hole is going to be big enough for other creatures to come in! We live here because creatures who would eat us can't get through this stone, but if you found a way in that—"

Calypso stops crawling and turns back to the frightened rabbit. "I told you, I swam. I didn't make the hole, it was already there."

"I thought you live in trees! Now you say you swim under the ground."

"You can go back and look for yourself if you want."

The rabbit is silent for a few moments. Calypso assumes he's going to check on the hole and starts crawling again.

"I'll believe you," the rabbit finally says, so close that it startles her.

"It was difficult for me to swim here and I can hold my breath longer than other creatures I've known," Calypso says. "If nothing else has ever come out of that hole before, I think you're probably safe."

The rabbit twitches. "Another sloth might come out of there."

"Not likely any would ever find the entrance or try, but I told you we eat leaves in the trees, so we won't bother you."

"What about the skreeks?" the rabbit asks. "Do they not eat you?"

"I don't know what that is."

"Kill-birds."

"Eagles," Calypso says. "Yes, they also eat us."

"They do?" The rabbit thumps the ground. "But don't they live in the trees, too?"

"Yes, but we are good at being hidden," Calypso says, "and we disguise our movements by being slow."

"Why are you here, then?"

"I'm trying to help my friends. There's another place like this one that's connected by the tunnel I swam through. My

125

friends are trapped in the other place by the giant monkeys and since I can hold my breath longer than them, I swam through to find some help."

"Sounds like you should hurry up, then," the rabbit says.

Calypso feels her temper rise. It's not a feeling she likes. "That's what I was trying to do before you started asking me so many questions."

"You were moving very slow before that."

"This is about as fast I can go."

"How do you not get eaten, then?" the rabbit asks.

"I told you," Calypso repeats, "we live in trees and disguise our movements by being too slow to attract attention. Yes, it's dangerous for us to be on the ground. My mother was killed by dogs when she was on the ground."

The rabbit's ears swivel up and forward, as though he is listening more closely to what she says. "I thought you said your friends are dogs?"

Calypso sighs. "Different dog and only one of my friends is a dog. I can't stay here and tell you the whole story—I need to get out of here to get help from Thundersloth."

"Who is that?"

"Thundersloth is an enormous smelly beast that the giant monkeys are using to fight for them," she explains, "but he doesn't like the monkeys and I think I can get him to help my friends."

"But you're so slow that it will take you a long time to reach anyone."

"I'll travel at night so I'm not seen by the day hunters."

"Then you have a while to tell me your story," the rabbit says, "because the sky fire is burning."

Calypso considers her options. "If you show me the way out of here and I find I have to wait for the sky fire to go out, I'll tell you the story."

"OK," says the rabbit, "but you'll have to dig the hole out."

"I don't really dig."

"With those claws?"

"They're for climbing trees, not ruining in the dirt."

"Hm," the rabbit ponders, "well, follow me."

Calypso follows the rabbit's footsteps past the doorway into another chamber where the shaft of light breaks through the far wall at the top of a pile of packed soil and debris. The rabbit runs up the slope into the shaft of light and turns around. "Stay down there and I'll dig it out for you."

"That's very nice," Calypso says.

"I want to hear this story and if you have to wait for dark, we'll have plenty of time for you to tell it."

As the rabbit digs, Calypso tells him the story of how she got there, leaving out much of the odyssey to keep it brief since he is making quick work of the hole. As she goes on, more rabbits gather around to listen. Well before she's done, the rabbit has finished enlarging the hole, and a clutch of rabbits sit around in rapt attention listening to the story of her and her friends.

Calypso climbs up into the warmth of the wide sunbeam and regains some much needed energy to continue her story. The curious rabbits ask her all kinds of questions about people, and how she came to be friends with people, and what it's like living high in the trees, what a boat is, and what it's like to drive one.

With daylight to burn, Calypso doesn't mind answering everything as best she can for these rabbits who have seen so little of the world, but the stress of the situation and the cold water and lack of sleep start to get to her. The rabbits eventually quiet down to let her rest for a bit.

When Calypso tells them how cold she had been, some of the rabbits lie down around her. Their soft fur, warmth, and friendliness is so comforting that closing her eyes for a moment immediately turns to outright sleep.

Calypso awakens to a cacophony of screeching, hooting, and banging coming from the direction of the big pyramid. Even with the sun behind some clouds, she has to shade her eyes with one of her hands and still can't see much. Shaking her head in annoyance at herself for not bringing the sunglasses, she climbs fully outside, followed by several rabbits.

"What's going on?" Digger asks her.

"I don't know. Maybe the giant monkeys are still fighting, or my friends are fighting back."

"Good," says another rabbit. "We don't like the aahks-hoots. They cut down all the trees that hide us from the skreeks."

Another rabbit with black rings around the bottom of her ears looks to the rainforest. "Is that it?" She hops a short ways up the side of the pyramid for a better look.

"Is that what?" Calypso asks.

"Is that Thundersloth?"

Calypso looks in the direction Black Ring is looking, but can't make out much. "I don't see well in the bright light and I can't see far, but he's very big."

"Bigger than a mule?"

"Much bigger."

"That's the monster that helps the aahks-hoots drag the cut-down trees and dig out the stumps afterwards," Black Ring says, "but I don't see any aahks-hoots or anything riding him."

"What's he doing?"

"Eating, it looks like. He eats trees, too?"

"Yes, that must be him!" Calypso says, then cries out to him, "*Aaaahhhhiiiieeee!*" She waits for a moment. "I can't tell, is he coming?"

"I don't think he heard you."

"*Aaaahhhhiiiieeee!*" Calypso calls again.

"Nope," the rabbit shakes its head. "Want me to tell him you're here?"

"You can't run over to him in the open during the day!" Digger says.

Black Ring comes back down the pyramid and stops a little past Calypso. A small flight of red macaws that look muddy green to the rabbits and would look black to Calypso if she could see them so far away, fly across the city. "I don't think any of the birds up there are the dangerous ones," Black Ring says. "I think I can make it."

"How can you even tell with how bright it is right now? You know they wait in the trees or fly really high up," A brown rabbit with a white spot on its nose says. "Don't do it, this is not our problem."

"Yes," Calypso says, "I don't want any of you dying for my fight. You're all so nice."

"And you didn't need to risk your life to help your friends," Black Ring says, shaking herself to get ready, "you could have stayed in the trees. It sounds like you all survived such incredible things because you work together and help each other."

Calypso looks at Spotted Nose, "I'd argue, but she's right."

Two more rabbits line up alongside the brave rabbit. "We're going, too. This *is* our fight if helping you means the aahks-hoots go away."

"I don't know that they'll go away," Calypso says.

"But you'll try," one of the new rabbits says.

"Yes."

"That's more than we can hope to do on our own."

The three rabbits take another scan of the sky, spotting a lone bird circling the ruins. "See that bird up there? You can tell it's a killer by the way it circles. It's looking for us, or baby goats, or anything else it can catch."

Calypso looks, but doesn't see anything. She squints and thinks she might see a black line in the sky.

"I can make it before the bird knows I moved," says a rabbit with white spots on its back. "It won't dare come near that beast."

"Then, we'll all run together. If there's three of us, it can only get one," Black Ring says.

"That one can be either of you," White Spot says. "I'm the fastest and I don't need you two slowing me down." With that, White Spot leaps from the base of the pyramid and makes for

Thundersloth so quickly that Calypso immediately loses track of him. Unfortunately for the rabbit, the bird doesn't.

It rolls over into a dive as the other rabbits at the pyramid look on in horror. The bird judges White Spot's speed perfectly and meets him with its talons at an angle, pulling him sideways and flinging him into a roll in the grass. The rabbits look away as the bird pins White Spot down and sinks its razor beak into him before flapping its wings and flying away with its meal. Calypso can't make out what happened that far away, but sees the rabbits' reactions.

"He didn't make it?" she asks.

"No," Digger answers sadly.

Calypso is silent for a moment. "Speed isn't always the best escape."

Digger and Spotted Nose look at her aghast.

"Sorry," she apologizes. "None of you should die for my problems."

"She's right," Black Ring says. "That's why we need to be thinking and working together like she did with her friends."

"Sounds nice, but how does that help us with this?" Digger asks.

Black Ring stands on her back legs, judging the distance to Thundersloth,, and then scans the sky. Another bird of prey patrols the city. Dropping back to all four feet, she nods to herself in thought, then looks at the other rabbits. "That looks like a small skreek. We run together zigzag, crossing past each other as we go. If we do that and the bird can still track us and drops on one of us, the other will be in position to give it a few good kicks and drive it away."

"Drive it away or not," says Digger, "if one of us gets hit, we're probably dead."

Black Ring nods solemnly. "But that bird would think hard about dropping on the rest of us again."

Calypso starts to climb down the pyramid. "I'll go," she says to the rabbits. "I don't want you two to risk yourselves for me."

"No, you said your friends might be fighting the aahks-hoots right now, so you all need our help." Black Ring turns to Digger, "Do you want to come with me?"

"No, but I'll do it."

"Good. High speed zigzag in loose formation. I'll lead."

He takes a deep breath, scans their path to Thundersloth, and nods. "Got it."

She leaps off the pyramid and Digger follows just an eye blink behind, crossing back and forth past each other as they rapidly span the wide field from the pyramid to the tree line. The bird tucks into a dive, but gives up halfway through, opening its wings, trading airspeed for altitude to get back to the wind currents. Oblivious to the quiet bravery heading in his direction, Thundersloth pulls down tree branches and strips off the leaves with his long tongue.

The rabbits both slow a beat and give an involuntary head shake when they get into smelling distance, but persevere through the stink to make it to the feet of Thundersloth.

"Hey!" Black Ring calls up to him, but he doesn't respond. "I forgot to ask if he speaks common," she says to Digger.

Digger cries out to get Thundersloth's attention and they both thump their back legs, but Thundersloth continues casually crunching leaves into a pulpy mash. A crowd of chimpanzees and several people hoot and shout a distance away near the large pyramid, easily drowning out the faint messages from the rabbits at his feet.

The rabbits try to get Thundersloth's attention again and this time Digger leaps up, spinning and kicking off of Thundersloth's leg. He spins again, and lands looking up at him. Feeling the kick, Thundersloth looks down on the rabbits curiously, still munching away.

The rabbits try to tell him about Calypso, but he doesn't understand what the tiny fluff balls have to say, so he goes back to eating.

Frustrated, Black Ring jumps up and hits Thundersloth's leg the same way Digger did and this time when Thundersloth looks down at them, she runs a short distance in the direction of the small pyramid and turns back to get him to follow.

Digger does the same and Thundersloth gets down and follows them a short distance before he hears Calypso's cry.

"*Aaaahhhhiiiieeee!*"

He's about to answer back, but looks toward the chimpanzees and decides not to. "*Ar,*" he gives a suppressed bark to the rabbits and tugs an old worn rope tying one of his legs to the nearest tree. The rabbits look at each other and nod, then run over and get to work chewing through the rope. Within a few short minutes, Thundersloth is free! Distracted by the fight, the chimpanzees don't notice him galloping away.

```
                  /\    /\                 ~ \   / ~
---------------  \ 0    0 / ------------------  (     )  ----------
                  \ /                            \_/
                   \/
```

The two chimps who would command them all exchange swings and jabs with spears—leaping, ducking, deflecting each other's blows while screeches and cheers erupt from one side of the circle or the other, depending on who they support. Papa and Lindo are evenly matched for a while, but Lindo soon shows signs of tiring in the heat of the sun.

Papa takes a long jab at him, purposely leaving himself open. Lindo takes the bait, thrusting the spear toward Papa's exposed chest. Papa dodges and grabs the shaft of the spear, pulling Lindo to him. Lindo tries to recover, yanking the spear back so that it slides through Papa's hand until the back side of the diamond-shaped flint spear point cuts into him, but he's too far off balance and Papa's extra strength pulls him in close.

Papa lets go of the spear and meets Lindo's face with his fist. Knocking him to the ground, he beats down upon his head with hammer fists. The noise of the crowd could drown out an exploding volcano as Lindo desperately puts his hands up to block the blows. In the midst of the Papa's relentlessly falling fists, Lindo summons the rest of his strength to shove Papa off of him and onto his back, expelling the air from the Papa's lungs.

Disoriented and bleeding from his head, for a moment Lindo stands and looks around at distorted faces, then blinks, wipes the blood out of his eyes, and picks up his spear. As he lifts it above his head for a killing blow, something knocks the breath from him and he tries to breathe again, but can't. His wide eyes look down upon a spear protruding from his chest.

With the last of his strength, he tries to stab Papa, but his vision goes black, his limbs go numb, and his own spear falls to the torn ground cover and mud with a quiet thump that bangs like a drum in the silence of the frozen crowd. Lindo drops to his knees and rolls over on his side. Blood covers the ground and spreads around him with his last struggle for breath.

Papa stands and picks up Lindo's spear, waving it as a challenge to the assembly. Some of the crowd starts to hoot. The opposing chimps screech, and then some begin to push each other and the pushing turns to blows.

Thundersloth's rider steps out of the crowd and cracks a whip at Papa, wrapping it around his spear, tearing it from his hands, and flinging it well out of reach. Papa hunkers down and bares his fangs in challenge. The rider screams back before leaping into the circle. The crowd quickly turns into a churning mob of shouting, clawing chimps engulfing Papa and his challenger, forcing them into a fight from multiple sides.

Miguel, Shriya, and Rondo back themselves against the pyramid, trying to stay out of the melee. Miguel watches their backs, thrusting at the few chimps that aren't too preoccupied with the battle to sneak up on them from above. Distracted by Miguel, the chimps don't notice Juan Manuel hop up the stones. With a crushing blow, he sends one rolling and bouncing to the ground, while the other scrambles across the pyramid to the front side.

The people try to hold off several charging chimps with spears while Good Boy mounts the pyramid to leap onto one moving on Shriya, catching the chimp's neck in his jaws, whipping the chimp around to fall and break his neck against the pyramid stone. Shriya impales another chimp before he can stab Good Boy, who immediately gets on his feet to attack another ape soldier that Miguel and Rondo are fending off, sending him into a stumbling retreat.

Chewed up and bleeding, the chimp crawls away. The remaining two turn back to the crowd. The people have held their ground against a small mob, but they're exhausted, bruised, and dehydrated. Rondo is bleeding from a heavy hit to the face and the earlier strike to the head. They only have one spear with a usable point left and its shaft is broken down to two thirds of its original length.

Papa and a few of his allies gather around the friends as the fighting dies down. Blood cakes Papa's fur, he clenches his hand to control the bleeding from Lindo's spear cut, and one of his eyes is swelling shut. Several chimps at a time drop their weapons and run for the jungle until about a quarter of them are gone, while pockets of fighting within the crowd peter out and a few more allies join Papa. The rebels now support the sloth rider, outnumbering Papa's loyal followers.

As they catch their breath and attempt to cool down, the wounded drag themselves away, and the allies gather useable weapons from the ground. Shriya tears off a sleeve of her shirt and ties it to Rondo's head to slow the bleeding. Miguel drops a few of the less broken spears he salvaged in front of them and pulls some of the dead chimps from the pyramid entrance so they can retreat inside and use the narrow doorway defense, if necessary. A strong breeze is welcome, but it's only of temporary help, and blows the foul stench of blood, death, fear, and sweat around.

Though the number of rebel chimps has been knocked down, enough remain to form up in a semicircle around the allies, blocking escape. Thundersloth's rider emerges from the crowd, dragging his whip, baring his teeth.

Good Boy stands to the right of Shriya, Miguel, and Rondo and the back stairs, and calls up to Juan Manuel pacing above them on the stones of the pyramid, surveying the whole scene with his wide-angle eyes.

"Hey, goat, get ready! When they attack, you come down those stairs and hit their flank. I'll hop up there while they're fighting the people and get over to assist you while the people and the chimps hold the center!"

Juan Manuel surveys the enemy line. "Won't they escape where it's open? We could both attack from your side, and we could all collapse the line from the end and drive them into the corner where the stairs extend out from the wall. If we jam them in there, their greater numbers won't matter."

"Now you're thinking like a killer human, goat!" Good Boy barks. "Earlier in the day, yes, but there's not much fight left in them. Give them an escape and they'll run like the others. Give them nowhere to go and they'll have to fight to their last breath."

Juan Manuel nods. Then, in the far end of his vision, he spots a large speeding shadow. "On second thought," he says, "I think I'll come to your side instead!"

"Stick to my plan!" Good Boy says, barking again.

"You don't see what I see!" Juan Manuel hops down next to Good Boy, who curses his stubborn friend. Thundersloth's rider raises his whip and lets out a horrible screech that vibrates Good Boy's bones. Then—*the smell!*

*Whoomp! Cra-crunch!*

The rider is violently yanked onto his back by his own whip and dragged backward, smashed into the ground by one of Thundersloth's giant claws. Propelled by Thundersloth's bellowing roar of rage, the enemy line instantly collapses in a panic of noise and fur. Two chimps go airborne in different directions, smashing into the pyramid with critical thuds.

"*Ar! Ar! Ar!*" Thundersloth barks a confident taunt at the panicking apes, now far too few and exhausted to overpower him. Too tired to run, a soldier tries to stab Thundersloth, but the chimp is off balance and the poor thrust barely makes a cut in the sloth's thick skin. Four angry claws skewer the chimp, which Thundersloth then tosses onto another who is foolishly charging him, slamming him backwards to the ground.

The remaining soldiers abandon their weapons and make a disorganized run into the rainforest. Thundersloth stands to his full height and raises his head to the sky.

*Ahhooooooooh!*" he calls in triumph, then turns to the cornered friends. Good Boy runs out in front of them, barking venom, ready to dodge his deadly claws in case he's still looking for a fight.

"*Aaaahhhhiiiieeee!*"

Good Boy stops barking and walks back a few steps. Of course, he thinks, who else? Calypso climbs onto Thundersloth's head and surveys the carnage in horrified awe.

"Calypso!" Shriya shouts, and the people drop their remaining broken weapons. Papa does the same and motions for his loyal soldiers to drop whatever weapons they have. Thundersloth snorts and drops onto all fours. Calypso climbs down his arm to Juan Manuel's waiting back.

Shriya rushes over and Calypso lifts her arms to be picked up, happy to see all her friends aren't among the bodies. Shriya smells bad, the men smell even worse, and the battlefield of torn chimps defies the limits of Calypso's vocabulary, but after Thundersloth, almost any other smell is welcome.

"What just happened?" Rondo asks, petting her head gently. "Did we get saved by a sloth again?" He stinks of blood, too. Calypso notices his head wrapped in a bloody cloth.

"Two sloths," Miguel says. "And one of them is supposed to be extinct."

"So are we. I guess it's just that kind of a day." Exhausted, Rondo as much drops to the ground as sits. "Oof, I'm feeling a little dizzy."

Shriya hands Papa the propeller spinner crown she's retrieved from the ground. He turns it over in his blood-caked, cut up hands and examines the scrapes and dents from the spear tip and its fall down the stairs and drops it to the ground without a second glance.

Shriya translates Papa to the people. "He says Papa is very sad. This is a bad day. This is a bad place. Friend chimpanzee kill friend chimpanzee like people. Is not good. Chimpanzee are not going to try to be like people anymore, they're going to act like chimpanzee and live in the forest."

The soldiers give subdued hoots and sign their agreement back to him. Shriya doesn't feel the need to translate.

Papa looks at Shriya and signs to her. "*People go to people home now and leave this forest to them.*" She signs back that they will tell nobody of them or this place.

"*Papa not care anymore. Chimpanzee no be here. Chimpanzee go far away. People can have people city.*"

"*Be careful,*" she signs.

With a toothy grin, he takes her hand and kisses it before heading for the rainforest with the soldiers in his wake. The soldiers don't look back, but Papa turns briefly and signs one last time before disappearing into the jungle.

"That's it?" Rondo asks.

Shriya holds her arms out to her sides and lets them fall. "They just want to be left alone."

"No problem there," Miguel agrees.

"Hey, look at all the rabbits!" Rondo says, standing up slowly and pointing to the large number of rabbits gathered around Thundersloth, eating vegetation and curiously surveying the scene of battle. "It looks like the lagomorphs shall inherit the city. Or do I just have a concussion? You all see the rabbits, right?"

Digger and Black Ring get within communication range of Calypso and thank her for getting rid of the aahks-hoots.

Calypso turns to them and gives all the credit to Thundersloth and her friends.

"Are they communicating somehow? Tell me you all see this so I don't think I've got major brain damage." Rondo says.

"No, we all see it. I wouldn't rule out brain damage, though."

"Funny," he frowns.

"That's about the least weird thing I've seen in the last few days," Miguel says.

"I half expect to wake up in the hospital and find out everything from the day I was picked up by a sloth driving a speedboat has been a dream," Shriya says, "induced by heat exhaustion after nearly succumbing to the sun on my broken Zodiac."

"What did the chimp king say to you at the end?" Miguel asks her.

"He said I'm the only human he'll miss." She looks towards the jungle. "I wish them luck finding where they belong."

"OK, that's very nice," Rondo says, "but now what do we do with the bodies of all these chimps?"

"Bury them if you want, but we're going home," says Shriya.

"I think I agree with Rondo," Miguel says. "After we get some water, we should bury them so they don't spread some kind of disease to the giant sloth."

Shriya sighs and looks around at all the bodies. "You have an excavator with you?"

Miguel purses his lips. "Maybe it would be easier to drag them into the pyramid and close it up again."

"Rondo, how are you feeling?" Shriya asks.

"I'll be OK with a little rest, as long as it doesn't get infected."

"Oh, I'm sure that sleeve torn off a shirt I've been wearing in a sweaty jungle for days is perfectly sterile."

"What about the giant sloth?" Rondo asks.

"What about it?" Shriya asks with a frown.

"It can't fit on the boat," Miguel laughs.

"It could be worth a fortune to prove these things are still alive out here," Rondo offers. "Maybe it's a whole new species they can name after you."

"It saved our lives, but even if it didn't, we're leaving it alone." Shriya's voice is quiet, but her eyes show that no disagreement will be entertained. "We'd also be betraying the chimps since anyone finding the sloth might find them, too."

"Now that this city has been half revealed, it's going to be found," Rondo pushes. "Might as well be by us than someone who will hurt it."

"Whatever someone else might do is beyond our control, but I won't be the one to exploit it. We'll leave here with our lives and be happy with that!" Now her voice matches the fire in her eyes. But Rondo doesn't back down.

"Do you think nobody else will ever examine those aerial survey photos and notice this lost city?" he says. "And when they come here—"

Shriya cuts him off. "With all the cuts to archaeology and competing finds in Europe and the Middle East that get more interest, it could be an awfully long time before that happens."

"I don't think so," Rondo says, "Now that these chimps have cleared so much of this area, some lone pilot might just happen to spot it from the air and tell someone. This thing may have been living unknown here for ten thousand years, but time's catching up to it."

"What lone pilot out here with no nearby settlements, much less an airstrip where no Mayan ruins are expected to be?" Shriya approaches him and glares. "If I can't trust you, when we're done moving the dead chimps, we'll seal you up in there with them. Maybe you'll be of interest to the next curious archaeologist who comes here."

Miguel glances at Shriya in surprise.

She matches his gaze. "I'm a paleontologist. I study these magnificent extinct creatures, trying to glean whatever we can from the few clues left behind. It seems likely that we were largely responsible for so many of the giant sloth's relatives going extinct, along with the demise of a number of other fascinating large mammals. I will not be the one who let it finally happen to whatever remnant population of giant ground sloth remains or stand for anyone else to do so, either!"

Shriya throws a pointed finger at Rondo. Picking up on her anger, Good Boy paces to her side, growls, and barks sharply at him. Juan Manuel faces Rondo with lowered horns, and, even though she has no idea what they're talking about, Calypso turns her head slowly around, holds her claws up in his direction, and aggressively opens and closes her mouth threateningly.

"Do *not* test me on this!" Shriya says in what sounds to Good Boy like a growl.

Rondo holds out his hands. "OK, OK, I just fought the war for the planet of the apes, I'm not looking to disturb the Pax Central Americana."

Shriya stares at him until he breaks his eyes away.

Miguel stands up and winces as some bruised and strained muscles voice their displeasure at his attempt at stretching. "How about we get some water from the well and move these bodies out of the sun before they out-stink the sloth?"

"It'll take an awful lot to smell anything over *him.*"

"He's not the only one who stinks," Miguel jokes, pulling his sweat-soaked shirt away from his chest, but nobody's in the mood to laugh.

"Maybe there's some food that's still good over there, too," Rondo offers. He attempts to stand and Shriya offers her hand to help him up.

He smiles. "So you're not quite ready to kill me yet."

"Don't push your luck, or your head," she tells him. "I'll help you get to some shade and Miguel and I will take care of the chimps."

"I don't want to push it," Miguel says, "but maybe we can get the mega death sloth to help us."

Shriya groans as she supports her lower back with her hand, and blows out a breath. "I'm not against asking nicely."

# Pyramid of the Moon

The stone ball clonks into place to seal up the tomb of the fallen former lab chimps, leaving enough room around the edges for insects and smaller animals to take care of the remains. Calypso is on Thundersloth's head and she scratches him in thanks for his help closing up the tomb. Shriya, Miguel, and Rondo sit in the shade at the edge of the rainforest and drink water from one of the wells in makeshift bowls through germ-filtering straws while their phones charge off of the solar chargers they got out of their recovered backpacks. Thundersloth lifts Calypso high up into a tree across from the small pyramid and she climbs onto a nice limb with some new leaves not too far out. Juan Manuel eats vegetation with the rabbits in the shade at the bottom. A hawk circles over the city, but doesn't dare dive on the rabbits with all the large animals so close to them. Just the same, they keep a safe distance from Good Boy, who returns from scrounging for fallen food on the wrecked market street to lay down to pant in the shade.

Rondo stares at the second pyramid, then shakes his head. "So, the sloth must have made it through that flooded tunnel and out the other pyramid, probably where those rabbits are going in and out. That could be why the rabbits are hanging around her. I wonder what's in there."

"The archaeologist sounds like he's still thinking about exploring," Shriya says to Miguel. "Maybe we should leave him behind."

"What's with the attitude?" Rondo asks.

Shriya scolds, "Her name is Calypso."

"OK. Fair enough, but you've been mad at me for most of the day," Rondo complains. "I already told you I'm not going to tell anyone about the giant sloth."

"I'm not angry at you. I'm angry at myself for forgetting why I broke up with you back in school."

"And how is that?"

"This stuff only means something to you on an intellectual level, not an emotional one," Shriya says, crossing her arms over her chest. "Your desire for knowledge for the sake of feeling superior is only exceeded by your desire to be famous."

Miguel winces, but is happy that Rondo is not competition after all.

"Who isn't in this to be recognized?" Rondo challenges her. "You came out here to look at the cave, hoping to be recognized for claiming the discovery of the most northern paleo cave ever found."

"No, I came here out of *curiosity* and because I'm interested to know the limits of the range of the ancient creatures who made them and to learn a little more about how they lived, maybe find evidence confirming it was giant ground sloths that made them, what kind, and why—even though they ranged well into North America—we haven't found any caves that they've made north of here." Shriya pauses and surveys the wreckage around them. "Now, in spite of the allure of finding possible solutions to some of those mysteries, I'm going to rest up and go back home. I'm not going to mention the giant ground sloth to anyone because I won't be responsible for it being killed or exploited. Whatever holdout population it is that he belongs to has been living here for at least the last ten thousand years, surviving indigenous hunters, early civilizations, Conquistadors, explorers, smugglers, looters, spy satellites, LIDAR mapping, and angry chimpanzees, so it stands a better chance by itself. Anything I could learn about it is less important than it being able to live its life in peace."

Rondo barely waits a moment before pushing his point. "Or you could make sure that you are in control of the inevitable expedition that will be digging this site because I can assure you that the next people that come along won't be so generous."

"Like you?"

"I already told you I'm not saying anything, but there's your vindictive streak—disagree with Shriya and she'll bite you and never let go."

Sounds like the way to be, Good Boy barks in agreement and puts his head back down. Rondo scowls at him.

"I've not known Shriya to be like that at all," Miguel says.

"You're either saying that because you still think you have a chance with her," Rondo laughs, "or you don't know her well enough."

"No, I think she's just that way with you because she cares about animals and you don't because you're a guineo."

"I don't know what that is and I don't care," Rondo says waving his hand as if shooing a fly, "Sit here and feel superior to me by pretending you're both some kinds of saints all you want. I know what I am." Standing, wavering a little with lightheadedness, he steadies himself, then unplugs his phone from the solar charger and heads for the smaller pyramid.

"I probably shouldn't have said anything," Miguel says quietly to himself.

Shriya gets out of a crouch to sit on the ground and extend her legs, exhaling in relief. "No, that's fine. You have the right to speak your mind the same as any of us."

"Yeah, but I shouldn't have kicked him while he was down. It's not like you need me to back you up."

Shriya smiles and kisses him on the cheek. "Sorry, my breath is gross."

"Mine's no better. And neither is my face."

"What I wouldn't do for a waterfall and some natural soap—even just soap for the next rain!" Shriya groans. "First thing I'm going to do when we get back is walk straight into the shower. Then I think I'm going to lay in bed for about a week . . . scratching bug bites. I'll even leave Calypso to tie up the boat!"

"I think I'll do the same. I hope the truck starts. The battery is . . ." Miguel shakes his hand to indicate that it's on its way out.

"Worry about the battery later."

"It's not up to me, it's up to the battery."

"If you end up stranded at my place," Shriya grins at him shyly, "I won't make you walk home."

Miguel looks into her eyes, pretty sure his heart will beat itself up against his rib cage. She breaks the gaze and he turns his head to stare unfocused in the general direction of the smaller pyramid, letting his mind wander on thoughts of her.

Shriya slaps his knee to snap him out of it. "Come on! Let's check on the jerk."

He really doesn't feel like standing up, but he clears his throat and rises to his feet as slowly as he can.

"Also, I don't like what you called him."

"Guineo? It's an unripe banana."

"We both know what it really means."

"I don't mean it like that. I use it like saying a man isn't a man, he's a coward."

"Then use that. Words mean what they mean. OK?"

He breathes out instead of arguing and rubs the back of his neck. "Yeah, OK."

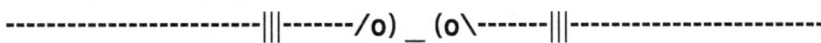

Calypso lays back in the split of two tree limbs, basking in a sunbeam, chewing leaves, and getting some much-needed energy from some hanging fruit conveniently within arm reach. Looking through her sunglasses at the ancient city, she thinks about how strange people are with their complicated interactions and the things they imagine and create.

Her eyes focus on the twig that the leaves she's eating stem from and it occurs to her that people might imagine something they could make with that twig, while she sees it as the parts of the tree that the leaves grow from as they reach for the sunlight. She doesn't need it to be anything else. Her mother taught her which plants to eat, how to survive the different weather, and which animals are dangerous.

People must teach their offspring how to make all these things, but how could they know so much? She munches some more leaves. She could teach her own offspring how to drive a boat, but why would they need to? Why do the people need to? There's no point to teach a young one how to drive a boat unless they could make a boat, too, and even she can't do that. There's no reason for her to know how to.

If she had never been involved with the people, she would have never needed to know how to drive, either. But the people saved her from the dogs that killed her mother, and knowing how to drive the boat saved Good Boy and Juan Manuel and the other sloth.

Calypso blinks her eyes and pulls another tasty fruit to her. Maybe Good Boy could have saved her from the bad men without the boat by jumping in the river, but then they wouldn't have found Juan Manuel, or the sad sloth where the people eat, and Good Boy wouldn't have been there to come back for help to save Shriya from the horrible chimpaneezees. Thinking about all this is making her brain ache.

Very dramatic lives, these noisy giants! That's why they must make so much noise and move so fast—they have so much to learn and do, even though it's all unnecessary. It seems stupid to make living so much harder than it needs to be. Calypso is glad she's a sloth, even though she knows she's not like other sloths. Living with people has made her do things no sloth has done or would even want to do, to think about things it's likely no other sloth has thought about, to work together with others to survive like no other sloth. The chimpaneezees spent a lot of time with the noisy giants, too, and started to become like them. If she spent more time with the people, would she become more like them, too? Maybe she already has. At least the chimpaneezees finally realized that it was dumb to try to be like the people even if many of them died before they figured it out. What a waste.

Head swimming from all the thinking, but finally warm again and with a full stomach, Calypso yawns and closes her eyes. The tree sways slightly as Thundersloth pushes on it to eat, and his smell rises up to overpower that of the rainforest, but she's getting used to it somehow. Flitting between being awake and dreaming about sleeping in a tree, she can only tell it's a dream when the smell is better.

Excited about all the interesting vegetation, Juan Manuel munches the plants growing along the edge of the rainforest. Catching sight of a hawk alighting on the pyramid, he gets the urge to scare it off before it tries to pick off one of the rabbits, so he finishes chewing and races over to the closest stairs. Leaping several at a time, he quickly reaches the summit, prompting the hawk to fly off.

Now able to appreciate the view without the threat of hostile chimpanzees, Juan Manual struts around the platform, eyes straining to take in the enormity of the rainforest stretching in all directions as far as he can see. He is the mightiest goat in all the visible land! The sounds of all the creatures blend together with one or two occasionally calling out over the din, their music channeled up the pyramid's sides. Birds of all kinds fly in and out of the canopy or glide effortlessly overhead.

Breathing in deeply, Juan Manual picks up the endless variety of wonderful scents. He spots the annoying person curiously digging his way inside the small pyramid, much to the displeasure of a bunch of rabbits that thump their back feet in ineffective protest.

Shriya and Miguel are talking nearby, obviously enjoying being so close to each other. Juan Manual shakes his head and wonders why people have such long and ridiculous mating rituals—why don't they just smell each other's urine and get on with it? Strange creatures. The annoying one finishes digging, Shriya and Miguel head over to climb through the hole in the pyramid with him, and Juan Manuel decides to head down to see what they're doing.

He ducks into the smaller pyramid and finds the people with their hand lights shining cone-like beams through the dark. They illuminate a bunch of carvings in the stone and the annoying person is using words Juan Manual doesn't much understand. All this new space and great smells and that's what they're looking at?

"Look who came in to check on us!" Shriya says.

"*Baahaahaahaa*," he says back, his tail wagging.

Rondo ignores Juan Manual and moves the light to explore the space. "Look!" he points to a path dragged through the filth on the floor. "This must be where Calypso crawled across. The tunnel must be this way."

Everyone follows him through a doorway into another room.

"Not much here," Miguel says.

"Must have been looted at some point," Rondo says, "like much of the sun pyramid."

"That's the bigger pyramid." Miguel asks with his tone more like a statement.

Rondo casts his light from ceiling to floor. "Yes, like I said before, the large one likely represents the sun and this one the moon."

"Some more statues," Shriya says.

"Yeah," he shrugs, training the light upon the floor at the other end of the room, revealing a hole. "What's this?"

Miguel leans forward and looks in. "I don't know, but I'm glad I didn't fall into it."

Rondo kneels by the edge and shines the light around. "Spaniards!"

"What?"

"Conquistadors." A smile crosses his face as he shines the beam along the small room below, then fades when he sees no obvious way in. "I wonder if they were left in this pit to die."

"Or fell in while looting," Miguel says.

The light clearly shows several intact skeletons still partially dressed in armor. The few along one wall look to have fallen apart. Rondo moves the light around and points at a pool of water on the floor. "Looks like this is the other end of that flooded tunnel. Calypso must have sneaked away to swim this and came up through here, then climbed up somehow. That's got to be thirty damn meters, all underwater in the pitch blackness! A *sloth* did this. Incredible. Simply incredible."

"She pilots a speedboat, came to our rescue *twice*, must have gotten to a lookout tower by herself . . . who knows how she even thought to do that never mind accomplish it. . . got by the chimpanzee guard on the tower without him noticing, and figured out how to use a zip line down to the pyramid," Shriya confirms. "This is all from an animal that evolved to live its entire life in trees within a small territory, moving at a maximum of three meters per minute. Oh, and she wears sunglasses that she puts on by herself and you think this is somehow more amazing?"

"It's all amazing. I'd be shocked by the dog doing any of it, though I'd believe it. If I didn't see what she could do, there's no way I'd buy it," Rondo says. "When sloths were first described by Western scientists, it was mentioned that they were so stupid that they wouldn't flinch when a gun went off next to them."

"They can't run and have little ability to fight, so their only real defense is to freeze and look like the background," Shriya defends her. "An animal that slow *and* stupid with fairly low reproductive rates could have never survived, would have never evolved that way in the first place! Never mind become so successful that they make up the majority of the large biomass in some areas of the rainforest. Tell me again who's the one who's stupid when those self-declared scientists didn't have the little bit of common sense needed to figure that one out?"

"Hey, you'll get no argument from me," Rondo mutters almost to himself..

"She probably climbed up this vine," Miguel interrupts, lightly kicking hanging, dead vegetation with a toe. "Or maybe it's an old root from one of the trees the chimps cut down. I guess sloths can see pretty well in the dark, if she found this. Someone told me they were practically blind."

"Root," Rondo says, shining the light on the path it takes across the floor and up into a small crack in the outer wall where it meets several more dead roots.

"They have rod vision," Shriya answers Miguel, looking at the skeletons and scattered bones below.

"What does that mean?"

"Our eyes have rods and cones," she explains. "The cones perceive color and can sense depth, but don't work in the dark. Rods don't perceive colors, but they pick up tiny photons of stray light to see in the dark. Sloths don't have cones."

"So they can't see color at all?"

"They might have some way of processing that we don't understand, but as we know it, their vision would be achromatic and grainy, with poor depth perception that would get overwhelmed by bright light," Shriya says. "They're also nearsighted and have a narrow range of focus, but I have my doubts about them being as nearly blind as some suggest. They evolved from the giant sloths, but the giant sloth has eyes on the sides of its head. Both families of tree sloths—separated evolutionarily from a common ancestor further back than dogs and cats—evolved to have their eyes on the fronts of their faces for binocular vision, which implies some kind of depth perception and, though their eyes are mainly meant for the dark, Bradypus like Calypso are cathemeral, not nocturnal as would be expected of an animal whose retinas only contain rods." Shriya stops to see if Miguel is following along. At his smile of encouragement and interest, she continues.

"Sure, the light and dark might not matter much if they navigate primarily by smell as is commonly reported, but the biggest reason I have my doubts is from watching Calypso. She seems to have limited vision, and she definitely doesn't like bright light, but she behaves as if she sees better than she should in situations where I can't imagine smell being a proper substitute. I think Pablo knew about her eyes and made her those sunglasses. It doesn't fix the other problems, but it probably keeps the bright light from washing out her vision as much."

Miguel shakes his head. "Who *was* that guy—the Slothman of the Caribbean? Beats the Birdman of Alcatraz for weird criminals."

"Criminal or not," Shriya says, "I would have liked to have met him. He obviously had a heart and his sister was very nice."

Miguel trains his phone light along the walls of the ground level room. "It seems strange that an animal that lives in trees would have such poor vision."

"Yeah, it's a mystery. The theory is that an ancient ancestor of sloths and anteaters lived underground and didn't need their cones. Why the genes for the cones haven't reactivated since then like most mammals . . .?" Shriya holds up her hands and lets them fall. "I guess they haven't needed them. The poor eyes and being slow probably just all resulted from adapting to a diet of limited energy. And with being so slow, it doesn't help to be able to spot predators that they can't escape. Instead, they just rely on camouflage and eating things nothing else wants to eat. That way, they also don't need to outcompete other animals for the same food source. You know, monkeys aren't native to the Americas."

"Neither are chimpanzees," Miguel interrupts to joke.

"No, and I hope they don't disrupt the ecosystem too much!" Shriya says. "We believe monkeys first arrived here somewhere over thirty million years ago. The Choloepus and Bradypus sloths evolved from a common ancestor about thirty million years ago. I've been wondering if competition with primates while sloths were taking over so many ecological niches drove the tree sloths to become such specialists that they essentially avoided conflict with the monkeys rather than trying to outcompete them, which they likely would have lost."

"Damn dirty apes," Rondo says in the voice of Charlton Heston.

"What do you think about the eyes of the giant sloth?" Miguel asks.

Shriya considers this for a moment. "We thought the extinct ones didn't have cones, either, but I suspect this one has them. I don't know if this one is a known or unknown ancient species, or an evolution of an old one that might have regained its cones."

"I think you are right," Miguel says. "It seems he can see OK in daylight."

"Yeah, it's one of the many things I'd like to study if we weren't going to leave him alone."

Rondo interrupts them. "As fascinating as sloth biology is, I'm going to go back out and get some rope so I can check out this hole."

"Climb the root," Miguel suggests.

"Yeah, I don't think that will hold me," Rondo says, walking back to the entrance.

"That's why I suggested it," Miguel says quietly.

Shriya smiles and hits him playfully on the shoulder.

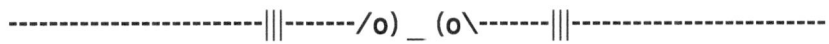

Juan Manuel watches Rondo descend into the pit on a rope. Shriya and Miguel brace against the doorway pillars while slowly letting out the rope to control his descent. Juan Manuel walks over to the edge and looks down as Rondo gets to the bottom and unties the rope to explore the hole.

"They look mostly undisturbed, though I think Calypso might have crawled over some of these guys while feeling her way along the wall. This one's head fell off." Rondo peers more closely at the skeleton. "Definitely Spanish Conquistador armor, but much of it is in a pile. Looks like they had taken most of it off . . . they might have been left down here to starve. I don't know why they put some of it back on, though. I imagine they were captured by whoever it was who had been occupying this city at the time." He pauses as he looks around some more.

"Yeah, see? This was originally a lower floor, much like the upper floor, except subterranean, and the original doorway to the interior of the pyramid is carefully packed in with blocks. I think they might have closed this place up and knocked a hole in the floor to make this into a kind of prison."

He examines the remains of the partially collapsed gateway to the tunnel of the dead and shines the light into the dark water underneath. "Ah, yup. It looks like the floor of the tunnel and part of this room collapsed after groundwater undermined the structure. Probably the same water we drank from the well, as gross as that thought might be. With all these blocks under the water here, I think this gate was also sealed off when these guys were in here, which would mean that this floor had fallen in sometime before they were interred here."

Nobody responds, but he doesn't expect them to. He kneels back down to look into the water. "There obviously must be a way through the tunnel that's at least big enough for a sloth, but I doubt there's much room to spare. Lucky her. Lucky us!" He shrugs to himself and turns to take a closer look around the skeletons.

"There are some bowls . . . small animal bones broken open for the marrow, probably. Maybe they were kept alive as prisoners for a while. I can't see any obvious signs of trauma to their bones, so I don't think they were killed, say, with arrows or something. Hey, I bet these stones that block the doorways came from the broken floor!"

"Maybe they were poisoned?" Shriya suggests.

"Could be."

"Maybe they put on the armor expecting a fight, but instead they were fed poison?" Miguel says.

"That's as good a theory as anything else," Rondo says, "but I think they were kept in here for a while due to the broken animal bones—hostages maybe? Could be they were waiting for a ransom that never got paid, then they were poisoned."

"Sure. It's probably impossible to prove anything at this point," Shriya speaks down to him, "but it sounds believable to me."

"It sounds believable to *me,*" Rondo responds haughtily, "and this is my area of expertise." He glances around. "I need to see what else might be here."

Juan Manuel walks around the interior of the pyramid looking for something more interesting than people talking. As he passes back into the entry chamber, stray light falls upon a goat monster lurking in the shadows.

"It's a devil!" he shouts as a general alarm, but, *"baahaahaahaah,"* is all the people hear.

Miguel's phone light moves toward the wall and Juan Manuel sees the shadow of the devil twitch at him. With a shot of adrenaline, Juan Manuel rears up and crashes his head into the monster. He's shaken by the force of the blow, but the devil is unmoved. Three steps back and he charges, catching it under its chin, but the devil holds its ground.

Unwilling to yield to the dangerous beast, Juan Manuel pushes with all his strength—his hooves cut through the dirt of the floor to grip the seams in the stone beneath, his muscles strain from his bones. With a pop and a crack, the monster starts to give ground, overwhelmed by his goat power. As a final defense, the beast throws dust into his eyes, but Juan Manuel blinks it out and pushes without relenting.

"*Bahahahahaha!*" he taunts it through clenched teeth. With a scraping, dragging sound, the beast slowly retreats into the wall. Victorious, he shakes his head and stomps his front legs, "Boom, devil!" Where's Good Boy?—a devil is no match for a goat! Hm, defeated monster smells funny."

"What's going on?" Shriya asks, a little worried at all of Juan Manuel's bleating.

"Charleston must have thought the statue was another goat or something because he attacked it," Miguel chuckles, "but look, he's found a secret passage!"

"*Statue?*" Juan Manuel scoffs, clacking his horns against the stone a few times with rising disappointment. "Hm, so it is. Well, don't I feel sheepish?" The pun would be lost on the people even if they could understand him.

"What's going on?" Rondo asks from the pit.

"Charleston pushed one of the statues and it opened up to a secret passage!" Miguel tells him.

Rondo stops taking pictures with his phone. "What? That's movie nonsense. The Mayans didn't do that!"

"Are you sure? Because, we're looking at one!" Shriya says.

"The scientists that said that aren't the same ones who said sloths are dumb or giant ones are extinct, are they?" Miguel asks.

"Or maybe the ones who say the Mayans didn't build cities this far south," she adds.

"We don't know these ruins are Mayan!" Rondo yells to Shriya's amusement.

"I think you should start making it a practice to push statues in these places." She taunts.

"OK, OK, well, help me up. I wonder if I could have discovered a whole new culture!"

"All by himself," Shriya whispers to Miguel, who nods his agreement.

All three of them walk through the newly open passage and shine their lights into the new room. Various objects of polished jade and black stone are piled against the far wall, reflecting the light—jaguars, eagles, snake heads, jewelry, and a small pile of conquistador armor in the far corner.

Rondo's excitement raises the pitch of his voice. "This hasn't been looted! We need to get a team back here."

"What about the giant sloth?" Miguel asks.

"He's avoided being discovered this long, I'm sure he knows how to avoid people." Rondo faces the two of them. "Look, I know what we agreed about leaving the sloth alone, but this is a major discovery!"

"So is the ground sloth," Shriya says, a menace in her words that even Juan Manuel picks up on.

"It is and I agree with you that we should let it be," Rondo pushes. "If we come in by helicopter, as long as it stays away from the site, it should be fine."

Shriya doesn't try to hide her incredulity. "An animal the size of an elephant?"

"He's stayed hidden this long!"

"Would you credit the goat with the discovery?" Shriya asks.

"I can tell that story after I get people back here with me," Rondo answers. "If I lead with that before anyone else sees this place, they'll just think I've lost my mind. In fact, I'll have to leave out most of what's happened if I want to retain any kind of credibility whatsoever. There are already enough crackpots in archaeology."

He takes some photos and shines the light down at two channels carved into the stone floor that run across the width of the room and end in two curved stone ramps that connect to the wall.

"This is strange," he says. "Look at these depressions in the floor leading to radiused buttresses against the outer wall. I've never seen anything like that in Mayan architecture before. They don't look like structural reinforcement. I wonder what they're for."

"The channels continue up the inside wall, too," Miguel says, shining his light on them.

"This place is really interesting." Rondo steps carefully over the first channel and onto the floor in between.

*Clonk! Fwoosh!*

Shriya yanks her arm away as two enormous slotted walls like halves of rock wagon wheels swing down from the right on pivots located at the tops of the channels in the inner wall and smash into it with a massive, cracking, echoing boom that hurts their ears and traps Rondo in the narrow space between the walls.

"Rondo! Are you OK?" she asks, coughing, through an impenetrable cloud of dust.

He answers, choking and hacking, while patting himself down. "For the moment. I think." He hocks up and spits hundreds of years of dead insect excrement and tries to squeeze through slots cut into the trap, but it's too tight.

Shriya shines her light at the bottom, showing some space between the floor and the trap. "Can you fit underneath?"

Rondo lays down and tries to squeeze under, but in spite of there being an indent in the floor under the trap walls, he can only reach his arm through. "No, and I'm nervous even having my arm under there."

"Maybe we should leave you in there so this place remains a secret."

"This isn't a joke."

"Who's joking?" Shriya says.

Miguel frowns and grabs hold of a slot, trying to pull the trap wall back. Rondo tries to help from his side. Shriya sighs and takes another spoke, but it's far too heavy.

"Well, that's not going to work," Miguel says, giving up.

Rondo rubs the top of his head, turning up a small cloud of dust, and looks down again. "OK, the floor under these things is lower than the rest." He knocks on it with his knuckles and it crumbles underneath and falls away. "Feels like ancient wood that's completely rotted—no lignin."

"Great," Shriya says, taking off her boonie hat and wiping sweat off her neck. "You still can't fit under it."

"No, but it's another interesting architectural detail." Rondo looks up and puts his back against one of the trap walls, stretching his legs across to the opposite one, and pushing himself up by sliding his back, then moving his legs up and repeating until he reaches the chambers in the ceiling where a gap exists between the top of the trap walls and the grooves where they fell out of the ceiling.

"Good idea!" Shriya encourages him. "Watch your feet—don't slip through the slots! Can you get over the top?"

"Not quite. There's a little more space than the bottom, but not enough to fit my head through."

"Well, you do have a big head!"

He sighs. "I walked into that one."

"Yeah, and the joke, too." Miguel smiles.

Rondo turns the phone back on and shines a light up the slot in the ceiling and into the top of the wall that the traps had smashed against. "It looks like the trap walls are on a giant pivot and these slots go way up above the axle the traps pivot from . . ." He shines the light into the slot above the other wall. "Yeah, it's both of them. And there are some kind of wedge-shaped stones above the axle."

He wipes sweat from his eyes "If those were to fall, they might break the stone bearing over the axle as it looks relatively weak. There are already some stress cracks and missing chunks in them that I'd guess comes from hammering the wall. I wonder if it originally would have had some wood to act as bumpers to cushion the blow? I suppose it doesn't matter now."

Rondo slips the light into his pocket, spans his arms across the walls to get his legs closer to the floor, and drops into a crouch, instantly regretting it with a shot of pain to his injured head. "I think there must be a way to release the wedges onto the pivoting sections of the walls so that they fall into the grooves cut in the floor. Then I'm sure I could climb over the top."

"So we need to find a trigger for the wedge stones?" Shriya asks.

"Yeah. This is pretty wild, huh?" he laughs, triggering another coughing fit. "Why would anyone build this ridiculous thing?" He spits out another lung's worth of filth. "This dust is brutal! I think I'm beginning to get an idea of what it's like to be a coal miner."

"You seem a lot less nervous than I would be if I was the one trapped in there," Shriya says, "though I certainly agree with you that this is very strange."

"For all the booby-trapped tombs in movies, the reality is not anywhere near as fun. Except for *this* one! It's unprecedented."

"I don't see anything that looks like a trigger," Miguel says, pushing on all the stones and statues.

"Ah," Rondo says with decidedly less enthusiasm than before. "I think I found it."

Miguel stops poking at the walls. "Where?"

"At the other end of the blocked off room behind me. There's a statue with an oddly outstretched arm that looks an awful lot like it could be a lever."

Shriya sighs. "Well, that's not going to work unless there's another way in."

"Nothing I can see unless there's a stairway hiding behind that old blocked up gateway the Spaniards are guarding, but I don't see a hole in the floor, anyway. Do you know where we can get an excavator?"

"I don't think even the giant sloth could move those stone blocks," Shriya says. "Too bad he can't fit through the doorway. We could have tried to get him to help move the wall."

"Even if it could, I'd die of the stink in this confined area," Rondo says. "If you can get me some kind of hammer-like thing, I might be able to break some stone between two slots in the wall. Though it might take a while. Or a piece of wing spar from a plane!" He looks at the small entry passage and the proximity of the wall and frowns. "Never mind, there wouldn't be enough space to use its leverage."

"I have something that could work," Shriya says, "but it's back at the boat, which means a couple days' turnaround."

"This is starting to seem a lot less fun now," Rondo says.

Juan Manuel looks through the slots at the statue in the other room, then shakes his head at the people—they're close, but not as smart as they appear to be. Rabbits scatter as he climbs out of the pyramid to take a quick look around before running toward Thundersloth.

"Calypso!" Juan Manuel calls up the tree.

Thundersloth snorts and pushes him away.

"Knock it off stinky! Calypso, we need your help in the rabbit mountain!"

Thundersloth stands up, grasps some leaves with his tongue, and pulls them into his mouth. Then he reaches up, shakes the tree slightly, and growls thunder.

A dog with three heads barks at Calypso from the back of the boat. She turns around and sees that the dog heads each have the horns of a goat. The strange creature laughs at her and she opens her eyes to find herself back in the tree where she had fallen asleep. The smell of Thundersloth tells her she's awake. She looks down through her sunglass lenses and blinks at his giant nose right underneath her. Having gotten her attention, he drops back to the ground and nods at a blurry figure that is probably Juan Manuel. She leans further to look.

"Calypso," Juan Manuel projects his thoughts with as much power as he can muster, "the annoying person is trapped in the rabbit mountain."

"OK."

"We need your help to get him out."

"Why can't the people help him?"

"They're too big to reach the thing!"

She blinks slowly. "What thing?"

"It's a monster's arm or something."

Calypso wonders if she might still be asleep. "What?"

"Don't worry, it's turned to stone. Come with me and you can see."

She waves a hand dismissively. "I don't even like that giant."

"Neither do I, but are we just going to leave him in there?"

"Yes?"

Juan Manuel continues to stare back up at her, not responding and not leaving.

Even with her nearsightedness, Calypso can tell he's still looking up at her, prompting a sigh. "OK, I'll help. Again."

It takes a minute of urging to get her exhausted body to respond, but she finally manages to start down the tree.

"Can you help her down?" Juan Manuel says to Thundersloth, nodding toward Calypso with his nose. "Do you even understand me?"

Thundersloth looks at him, then to Calypso making her way down the tree, then back at Juan Manuel. Then he stands up with no sense of urgency.

Juan Manuel brings her back to the pyramid and up to the entrance. "Where's Good Boy?" he asks.

"Still sniffing out food, I think."

He blows a raspberry in disappointment. "I wanted to show him something."

"You have better eyes than me. Do you see him?"

He scans the grounds. "No. Let's go in." They go inside the pyramid and he jerks his head toward the goat statue. "Don't worry about that devil, it's just stone."

"Yes, I can tell."

Shriya's face lights up upon seeing Calypso. "Yes!—she can sneak between the slots in the walls!"

"How do we get her to understand that she needs to pull the statue's arm down?" Miguel asks.

"We don't even know if she can move it in the first place," Rondo says.

"Maybe not," Shriya says, "but you don't think it's amazing that Charleston went to get her all by himself to help?"

"At this point, I wouldn't be surprised if a flying saucer landed outside and a drunk werewolf stumbled out to give me tickets to a zombie Elvis concert," Rondo mutters.

"What are they saying?" Calypso asks Juan Manuel.

"No idea, but do you see the stone monster through the slots?"

She lifts her sunglasses, which are of little help in the dim pyramid, and stares through the trap walls, but only sees a blurry figure that might be it. "I don't know."

"Well, there's a monster made of stone in the room with its arm stretched out."

"OK. Are you sure it's been turned to stone?" Calypso asks.

"Of course! With all the rabbits in this place, you'd see their bones everywhere if it wasn't."

"Good point," Calypso agrees. "So what do I have to do to free this person so I can get back into the trees?"

"You have to push it or something." Juan Manual nods to the statue that had hidden the room. "I found this room by pushing on that stone devil."

"Why did you push it?"

"Well, I . . . I thought it was that devil thing Good Boy and those bad people talked about a long time ago."

She eyes the statue again, this time with suspicion. "Are you sure it isn't? There are crunchy creatures that look just like sticks. You'd never know if you didn't see them move. What if it's a devil that looks like stone?"

Juan Manuel looks at the statue carefully for a few moments. "No, I'm pretty sure it's stone. People said it was and they made this place, right? They probably made these monsters, too."

"That's silly, why would they make monsters?"

"Why did they turn lab dogs into big monkeys?"

"I'm pretty sure they didn't," Calypso says.

"Well, somebody did!"

"They're just big monkeys. The only ones that made them were other big monkeys."

"But, how do you know?" Juan Manual asks.

She slow blinks again. "It's just like when the female goat and the male goat get the urge to get together and the male goat—"

"I know how that works!"

"You asked how I knew where the big monkeys came from," Calypso says, "well it's the same as the rest of us."

"I meant, how do you know the people didn't make them out of dogs?"

"What about the stone monster?" she asks, changing the subject.

"I'm thinking the people might not have wanted anyone finding this room, so they made this monster to scare anyone away from getting in."

"Maybe it's a hiding place from jaguars," Calypso says.

"Maybe."

She looks at the blurry shape through the slots in the trap walls. "How am I going to move that one? I'm not as strong as you."

"You're the only one that can fit through these slots."

"OK, but that doesn't do much good if I'm not strong enough to move the monster."

"Just go take a look or something," Juan Manuel tells her.

"I should have stayed in the tree," she says, sliding off of him.

Rondo picks up Calypso as she climbs through his prison and moves her to a slot in the second wall. Grabbing hold of the other side she looks at him with annoyance before slipping through and climbing to the floor.

"It's all true, isn't it?" a small and nervous voice asks Calypso from the shadows.

She turns her head in the direction of Digger. "What is?"

"Your stories. I didn't believe them because you're so slow, but you rode in on top of the goat."

"Why would I say it if it wasn't true?"

"I don't know. To seem scary? Predators might not mess with you if they think you're dangerous."

"A jaguar tried to eat me once and it never asked for a story," Calypso says. "The dogs that killed my mother didn't, either. Have you heard predators ask for a story? If you tell a good enough one, do they let you go?"

"Not that I've ever seen."

"Then why would I do that?"

"Well, you were surrounded by us, so maybe you were making sure we wouldn't attack you."

"You're rabbits," Calypso says.

"We can be pretty mean sometimes!"

"Sloths avoid predators by not being noticed at all, not by trying to be scary."

"How did you escape it?"

"Escape what?"

"The jaguar!" Digger asks impatiently.

"Good Boy and Juan Manuel fought it off and saved me."

"A jaguar? Those are some friends!"

"They are the best friends," Calypso says.

"Are the people your friends, too?"

"The female one is and the male with her is OK. Good Boy doesn't like him, but he treats Juan Manuel nice and I like him."

"So, what are you doing now?" Digger asks.

"I have to push this stone monster over there so that annoying person can get out from being stuck and I can go back to the trees."

"Yeah, I saw that. And *heard* that—hurt my ears!" Digger says, his nose twitching. "Those walls came smashing down. It was very loud, shook the whole place. It's good for him that he didn't get crushed."

"That would definitely make a smelly mess."

"I don't like the people being in here," Digger says "Do you want any help?"

"Sure, I don't know what I'm supposed to do, but maybe we can figure it out together."

Digger steps out of the darkness and hops over and they sniff each other, then the rabbit looks at the statue. "Is that the stone monster?"

"It should be. See the arm sticking out?"

"That's an arm?"

"Whatever it is that's sticking out," Calypso says. "Do you see it?"

"Yes."

"I'm going to try to climb up."

Digger runs impatient circles around Calypso as she crawls. "What can I do to help? Can I pull you along?"

"I think you're too small to pull me without getting hurt."

"What's going to happen when you pull the arm?" Digger asks, hopping in front of her. "How is the person going to get out of there?"

"I don't know."

"That makes me nervous," Digger says.

"You don't like the person being trapped in there."

The rabbit looks at Rondo and listens to the echo of the people talking. "Definitely not."

"Well, then why fear the change?" Calypso asks.

"I'm always afraid of change!"

"You would prefer something to stay bad than maybe get better?"

"It could also get worse!" Digger says, standing still for a moment.

"Yes," Calypso agrees, "but it will always be worse when you look at it in fear."

"How else would I look at something scary?"

"Like an opportunity to adapt and learn something new. The more you learn, the easier it is to adapt to change."

"That sounds wise," Digger says, "but I don't know if it really is."

"Maybe it isn't. Most sloths think I speak nonsense when I say things like that, but Juan Manuel told me that there's a comfort for group animals in not knowing the truth if it's bad, even when it's dangerous not to know." Calypso doesn't speak for a moment, but she keeps climbing. "For me, knowing things is comfort, but maybe believing something they would like to be true even if it isn't is a comfort for group animals. Or maybe that's just for the sheep he was talking about, I don't know."

"What are sheep?" Digger asks.

"They're a bit like goats, but also different. It's not important."

Calypso reaches the statue, then carefully feels out places to grip to climb up. Reaching higher, her claw catches in a gap between the statue's arm and shoulder, which she inspects and determines that it might be a separate piece from the rest of the statue. Juan Manuel must have been right about what the people said, but she doesn't know how to work it. She decides to climb out onto the arm like it's a tree limb and see if she can figure something out.

As she gets to the end, the arm starts to drop and one of the people shines a light on her—annoying, but not strong enough to dazzle her vision at the distance.

"That's it!" Rondo says, his voice a booming echo in the room. "There was a noise from the stone wedges!"

"Yeah, but even if that does drop the stones," Miguel says, "she's at the end of the arm and I don't think she weighs enough to bring it down all the way."

Shriya squints into the darkness. "Is that a rabbit standing by watching her?"

"Looks like it," Miguel agrees.

"Isn't that funny?"

Calypso extends herself as far as she can off the end of the arm, and hangs. The arm moves a little more, but stops.

"You hang upside down!" Digger remarks.

"Yes."

"You don't climb on top?"

"Sloths hang."

"Interesting. Can I help?"

Calypso turns her head around to face him. "I don't know. I think we need to bring this arm down, but I don't think you're heavy enough to make a difference. Maybe if I had a vine . . ."

"No, but I can thump it as I jump off of it. That might be enough to knock it off."

"We're trying to bring it down, not knock it off," Calypso says, "but that's worth trying. Can you jump way up here?"

"Let me show you!" Digger runs in a circle around the room to build up speed and Calypso can barely track his movement before he leaps up to the statue's body, uses it to hop onto the arm and launch himself into the wall behind. He turns his body mid-air to hit the wall with his back legs, then kicks off it to land on the floor in a sliding halt and fog of dust.

Calypso can't even turn her head before the arm drops from the blow of Digger's legs. She tries for a better grip, but her back legs slip off, and she lands on her shoulder on the floor to a tremendous crash that echoes and reverberates through the room, then two louder, deeper crashes vibrate the entire pyramid followed by a shockwave of air filled with crumbled rock and dirt. Peppered with small pieces of stone with her head tucked into her chest and arms, Calypso holds still and hopes the entire place doesn't come down around them. When it doesn't, she lets the dust settle for a bit before peeking her head out to see Juan Manuel staring at her.

"You did it!" he exclaims. Then he sneezes.

"How did that happen?"

"I don't know, but it worked." He sneezes again and coughs.

"The rabbit helped."

"I saw—those were moves that would make a goat proud."

The people cough and hack in the background.

Calypso sneezes and picks up her sunglasses, which had fallen off. "Can you take me back to the tree now?"

Juan Manual lowers his head. "Climb on up."

Calypso grabs his horns and he lifts her onto his back. Miguel, Rondo, and Shriya gather around the two of them. Shriya pats Calypso's head and removes her sunglasses to try to blow off the dirt, but it's of limited effect and Shriya's shirt is too dirty to be of any use. Instead, she helps fix them back onto Calypso's head. Miguel and Rondo smile at her.

"Thanks, Calypso!" Rondo says. "You've got to be the most amazing sloth that's ever lived!"

She looks around for Digger to credit him as a helper, but he's disappeared. Smart—the best thing about being fast isn't the ability to escape predators, it's being able to escape social attention.

Juan Manuel steps over the top of one of the walls where it had fallen most of the way into the floor and looks through the settling dust at the broken trap walls reaching up like ramps into pockets in the wall and ceiling. These ramps lead to the chisel-ended breaker stones that are now sitting on top of the axle that the trap walls had hung from, continuing the ramps started by the trap walls and extending far into the ceiling. Deep indents are cut across the surfaces of what used to be the tops of the trap walls as well as the breaker stones set like foot holds to make them easier to climb. Juan Manuel and Calypso's eyes follow the stones into the darkness above until Rondo comes over to shine a light up them.

"Well, can you believe this?" he says, "the walls and the breaker stones have grips carved into them almost like rungs on a ladder."

Miguel peers up cautiously. "You can go up first."

Rondo looks at Shriya. "No, ladies first!"

Juan Manuel blinks at Calypso. "I want you to know that I'm going to have to climb that. I mean, there's just no way I can*not* see what's up there! Do you want me to bring you back to the tree or hang on?"

"Do you really have to ask a fellow climber?" Calypso asks. "Onward and upward, goat!"

"Hang on tight." While the people joke and argue about who should go first, Juan Manuel tests the stability of the fallen trap wall with his front legs, then he ducks and scrambles up and into the blackness.

The air is very stale and even more surprisingly dry than the lower floor. The shaft of light coming from Rondo's phone light below is plenty enough to adequately illuminate the broad outline of the room, which is smaller than the one below, with sloped walls on three sides. Something on the wall opposite the entrance reflects back at them threateningly.

"Could those be teeth or eyes shining at us?" Calypso asks nervously.

"I hope neither," Juan Manual says, "but they're not moving, so whatever it is might be dead."

"I don't hear any goat screams and the pyramid isn't collapsing around us, so I guess it's safe," Rondo says, but Shriya is already halfway up the other ramp.

"Leave it to someone who studies extinct monsters to out brave the one who studies extinct cultures," Miguel says.

"Where does that leave you?" Rondo asks, but Miguel is already scrambling up the ramp behind Shriya. Rondo brings up the rear.

When the people emerge from the cavities and shine their lights upon the piles of stuff, Calypso and Juan Manual still don't know what they're looking at, but they can see that it isn't a monster, dead or otherwise.

"Conquistador armor," Rondo remarks excitedly. "Some of it still has a little shine to it!"

"They don't make it like they used to," Shriya jokes.

"Cosplayers and reenactors don't need that level of quality." Rondo says, tapping at it. "Looks like much of it has a little more than surface rust. Still impressive for being hundreds of years old."

"There's a lot of it," Miguel observes solemnly.

"Look at the dents in them," Shriya points out. "And the holes."

"Yeah, whoever these originally belonged to didn't take them off to go to bed." Rondo repeatedly pulls and releases his shirt to draw air across his chest. "It's strangely—*refreshingly*—dry in here and that must have helped preserve them."

"Is that all jade?" Miguel asks, shining his light on the side wall at piled statues of green stone.

"Yup," Rondo confirms, glancing disinterestedly to turn his attention to a small brass box peeking out from under some of the armor. He kneels down and looks carefully around the armor pile with his light.

Juan Manuel sniffs the pile.

"What is this stuff?" Calypso asks him.

"Some kind of clothes, I think."

She reaches out and taps one with a claw. "Seems like it would make moving difficult."

"Probably stop a jaguar's teeth, though."

She nods. "Like a turtle shell. Good point."

"*Bad* point," Juan Manual says, pointing his chin at a large puncture mark on a breastplate. "Do you think that was from the stink sloth or the giant monkeys?"

"Probably the chimpaneezees blocked them in like they blocked us in the other hill."

"They're just chimpanzees," Juan Manuel says.

"Tell me about it—they might be dangerous, but us sloths taught them they're no people!"

"No, I mean they're just called," Juan Manual starts. "Never mind. Or maybe it was other people who did this? Before the chimpanzees, I mean."

"Maybe," Calypso says, "but why would they use those pointy sticks when they have the sticks that shoot those stones . . . what are they called?"

"Bullets."

"No, that's not it."

"Guns?"

"Yeah, guns."

"Guns are the sticks," Juan Manual says. "Bullets are the stones that fly out of them. It could be that those holes were caused by bullets, but people have all kinds of terrible weapons. I don't know why they pick one over another."

"Maybe it's like I don't always want to eat the same tree leaves," Calypso says. "Cecropias are my usual favorite, but it's nice to have a variety."

"Yeah, I guess for people it gets boring killing each other the same way all the time."

Calypso blinks at the pile. "That looks like a lot of dead people. The rainforest must have been quieter for all the rest of us after that."

Juan Manuel bleats out a laugh, prompting Shriya to pat his head.

Calypso turns away from the armor pile to the stack of jade statues. "I don't understand how they can make so many things and still kill so many of each other."

"Look what we've done because we worked together," Juan Manuel says. "People are smarter and this is what they can accomplish even though they also kill so many of each other."

"That's what I mean—I'm wondering how much they could do if they didn't kill each other all the time."

"There also doesn't seem to be much that eats them, so maybe there'd be too many of them if they didn't kill each other," Juan Manuel says. "I heard a story about a small land with no killer animals where goats ended up. They bred and bred until they ran out of food and they all starved to death."

"How did you hear that?" Calypso asks.

"Goat lore. I don't know where it comes from."

"Are you sure it's true?"

"Of course not," Juan Manual says, "but the important part is the lesson in there."

"Not reproducing so there's enough for the rest?"

"More like, the importance of killers. They need to survive by eating some of us so the rest of us can have enough to eat. It's about the balance of nature. Like you keep the trees in check by eating the new leaves."

"Oh, yeah, and people are their own killers." Calypso scratches her head. "But they don't eat each other, so they don't have to kill. No, I think some of them are just bad. And even with killing each other, they're still everywhere." She closes her eyes and shakes her head. "And sooo noisy."

"It's not like the rainforest is quiet without people," Juan Manuel says.

"No, but the people noises don't fit. They can live anywhere else."

"Maybe *that*'s why they kill each other—they annoy each other too much!"

"That seems excessive," Calypso says, "but people are excessive."

Rondo manages to slide the box out from under the armor without disturbing anything much and examines it. It's 30 cm by 60 cm, and 5 cm tall. Wiping the lid with a sweaty shirt reveals a colored ceramic inlaid flag with a jagged red X on a white field covers most of the lid. His hands shake from excitement.

"This is the Spanish Cross of Burgundy! I wonder if the original owners of this armor had taken over the city and then it had been retaken," Rondo says, kneeling back down in front of the box. "Get back a little bit in case there's some kind of booby trap. After what's happened already, I don't want to take any chances."

Miguel and Shriya step back and Rondo feels around the box to make sure there's no trigger mechanism, then he carefully lifts the lid with the opening pointed away from everyone. Nothing happens, so he removes the lid. A lip around the inside edge fits snugly inside the box. Some symbols and words are engraved into the underside in old Spanish. Rondo sets it down carefully.

Miguel shines a light on a book with a dried out and cracked leather cover inside. "Where's the gold? We've found the clever traps and a treasure chest with an X on it, shouldn't there be treasure?"

"Probably all loaded onto a ship for inbred King Charles to squander," Rondo says.

"That story sounds fun, but I am still disappointed."

"After all the amazing things we've seen?" Shriya questions.

"I know! I feel like a spoiled child, but when I saw that box, all I could think of was a treasure chest," Miguel says. "I've seen too many movies. Eh, it is too small to have enough treasure."

"Small or not, it would be a nice end to this adventure," Shriya agrees, watching as Rondo tries to read the fancy ink script on the top paper of the book.

"What is it?" she asks.

"Not sure. It might be a logbook." Rondo looks around and finds a chip of stone under the pile of armor, which he uses to lift between the leaves of ancient parchment, reading the repetitious lines of words and numbers. "Ha! Do you see that name right there?" He points at something on the first page.

"What about it?" Shriya asks.

"This is the logbook from the *Santa Teresa de Avila*!"

"What is that?"

"She was a famous treasure galleon that was lost in a hurricane," Rondo explains. "Little is supposed to have been recovered by Spanish salvagers and pirates who raided the salvage camp."

Miguel takes a step back. "Pirates?"

"Yeah, according to the legend and some known facts, the *Santa Teresa* and three other ships were loaded and waiting for men-of-war to escort them to Cartagena, but the gunship escorts were delayed when they had to quell a native uprising, so the treasure ships were loaded with additional cannons, given a few smaller auxiliary ships for backup, and ordered to sail because the War of Spanish Succession was in full swing and the crown needed the money."

Rondo looks at the ancient page again, then continues his story.

"Instead of going from Portobello to Cartagena, they were to sail straight to Havana to meet up with a larger fleet for the trip back to Spain. However, luck wasn't on their side and the fleet was overtaken by a powerful storm. The *Santa Teresa* was driven into the shore and broken up by the waves, while the other ships were able to keep off the rocks. One of the surviving auxiliary ships, having thrown their cannons and ammunition overboard to keep her upright in the storm, largely demasted, and practically drifting with very little improvised sail area left, became easy prey to the pirate, Louis LeFleur."

"Who is that," Shriya asks, caught up in the story now.

"Louis is mostly remembered as an associate of Captain Robert Williamson, but he was a pretty scary guy in his own right. Through interrogating the Spanish crew and from those who joined his pirate gang, LeFleur found out about the wreck of the *Santa Teresa* and its approximate location," Rondo narrates. "Transferring whatever he could find of value on the auxiliary ship to a large sloop in his fleet under command of his First Mate, he then set out to find the wreck and attack any salvage operation that may have been on the scene. LeFleur sailed the coast until he found the salvage party and killed everyone who didn't escape into the jungle."

Rondo glances at the pile of armor, and Shriya and Miguel follow his gaze.

"What happened after that?" Miguel asks, feeling a chill along his spine.

"According to the Puritan minister, Cotton Mather, who claimed to have interviewed some pirates who were later caught off Cape Cod and had sailed with LeFleur and Williamson, the salvage operation was supported by a settlement and a small fort that had partially collapsed into the sea in the same storm that sank the *Santa Teresa*," Rondo says. "If that's true, then there might be some kind of remains that would make it easier to locate the treasure."

"But LeFleur already got the treasure," Miguel says.

"Well, even if there was a recovery operation going on and he was able to recover salvaging equipment from the Spanish, I doubt he was prepared to engage in underwater salvage and risk being caught by reinforcements from the Spanish Navy, so he probably got whatever had already been recovered by the salvagers and left the rest to the sea." Rondo sighs and caresses the box.

"We'll never know. LeFleur joined up with Williamson's pirate fleet shortly after, and his ship was lost with all hands in Williamson's first large battle with the British. Owing to the rather primitive salvaging capabilities of the time, it's likely that much of the treasure is still in the area of the wreck. People have been looking for centuries, but nobody's sure where it ended up."

"What did they have for salvaging equipment back then?" Shriya asks.

"Mainly diving bells and the skills of any local pearl divers."

"They had diving bells way back then?"

"Oh, yeah, early versions of them date back to at least a few hundred years BCE," Rondo affirms. "At the time of the *Santa Teresa*, they even had some with windows and an air supply that could be replenished by dropping down weighted barrels of fresh air."

"*That* long ago?" Miguel shakes his head. "You know a lot about pirates, too, huh?"

"I've been fascinated with the golden age of piracy ever since I was a kid," Rondo says. "It was what originally led me to archaeology and Williamson is one of my favorites—really more of a Scottish freedom fighter than a pirate."

"Sounds like revisionist romanticism," Shriya says. "As cool as the idea of pirates might have been, I'm more likely to believe Williamson was a bloodthirsty criminal.".

"As they say, history is written by the victors, and that's the story they told. Closer to the truth is that Williamson was originally a privateer given letters of marque by the British crown to hunt French ships and pirates." Rondo looks at the armor again, and smiles.

"At some point, he came across an incompetent British Naval captain who had navigated his ships into the doldrums and used up much of their supplies while waiting for the wind to return. The captain tried to impress Williamson's men to make up for those of his who had died or were too weak to work. Unfortunately for the British captain, Williamson had a galley, which allowed for oars, so he fled in the night and, knowing he would be pursued by the Navy for doing so, turned outright pirate and began hording treasure in order to save and build up a floundering Scottish colony in Panama. It was said that the value of the treasure within the hold of his flag ship, *Duchess*, alone would have been enough for the colony to build a fleet of warships that could have challenged for supremacy in the Caribbean and, perhaps, been able to support Scotland against English hegemony. Obviously, that didn't happen because Williamson was eventually killed in battle with the British Navy and Scotland became part of the Kingdom of Great Britain in 1707."

"Interesting to wonder what would have happened if that was true and he was able to succeed," Shriya says.

"Maybe India wouldn't have been colonized," Rondo offers.

"I don't know. I think with the trade interests of the time, the weakening of the Mughal Empire, and the strength of the East India Company, it might have only delayed the inevitable, but in the Caribbean?" She shrugs. "Who knows?"

"Wow, I really feel like the dumb kid in class," Miguel says.

Rondo glances up at him. "That must be a comfort."

"Yeah, it also reminds me of hanging with the smart kids and beating up on their bullies," Miguel says. "I loved beating up bullies!"

"Well, everyone needs to find a way to be useful. If you can't wield the hammer, *be* the hammer."

Shriya rolls her eyes. "OK, can we come back from the playground now?"

"What are they saying?" Calypso asks Juan Manuel.

"I don't know, but it seems like the annoying one is issuing a challenge to Miguel so Shriya will choose to mate with him."

"Why does she have to choose one of them?" Calypso asks.

"In this case? Because one is that annoying guy, but he still thinks he has a chance."

Calypso chuckles silently. "Miguel would definitely push the other one out of the tree. She's either choosing Miguel or neither of them."

"I don't think the other one knows that."

"In some ways," Calypso says, "the noisy giants are not smart."

"It might just be that they're so much more complicated."

"But they're the ones making it complicated."

"OK, so this is not so interesting anymore," Juan Manuel says. "You want to go back to the trees?"

"Always."

They return to find Good Boy laying in the shade at the edge of the woods upwind from Thundersloth and a tall tree's height worth of length away.

"Where have you been?" he asks with a yawn, his pink tongue curling between his incisors.

"In the other stone mountain," Juan Manuel says.

"Is it just like the first one?"

"No, you missed an adventure."

"Yeah, sure," Good Boy says doubtfully, laying his head back down.

"It was," Calypso insists. "The annoying—"

She stops at noticing the rabbits coming over to listen and waits a moment for them to gather before starting again.

"The annoying person got stuck between huge walls with holes in them and I had to climb through because nobody else could fit and one of the rabbits helped me knock down the arm of a devil thing that turned to stone."

"That one wasn't a devil," Juan Manuel says.

"I think it was."

"No, I don't know what it was," he says again, "but the other one was a devil."

"Whatever it was," Calypso continues, "its arm dropped, the walls crashed down through the ground and the annoying person was free. Then we climbed the top of one of those walls into a room in the canopy—"

"There was no way to get into the room when the walls were up and the room where that person got trapped was hidden, too," Juan Manuel adds.

"That's right. Juan Manuel found the first room by pushing another monster that got turned to stone that was blocking the entrance."

"But I didn't know it was guarding the room—I just saw it make a threatening move and I rammed it!"

Good Boy looks back and forth at the two of them. "What?"

"It's true! It was that devil thing," Calypso insists, with a slow nod.

"I think the people made that devil," Juan Manuel says. "I'm not actually sure it was ever alive."

"Yeah, but you saw it move?"

"I think so. It looked like it moved. Maybe it turned to stone when I hit it, I don't know. The people said it was a statue."

"Maybe they turned it into a statue. If people can turn lab dogs into giant monkeys and back into dogs, why not turn devils into statues?" Good Boy asks.

"That's kind of what I was thinking," Juan Manuel agrees.

Calypso shakes her head, but doesn't bother to argue as they're going to believe what they want to believe, either way.

"So what was in the other room?" Good Boy asks.

"Some turtle clothes from dead people, and a box with some stuff in it that the giants use to tell each other things without having to talk," Calypso answers.

"The what?" Good Boy asks.

Thundersloth sticks his nose in and nuzzles Calypso. The rabbits scatter into the ground cover.

"She means paper," Juan Manuel says.

"What *is* that?" Calypso asks Juan Manuel, scratching the thin fur behind Thundersloth's nose.

"I think it's made from trees," he says.

"Are you sure?" Calypso asks. "That sounds ridiculous."

"I think it's really thin bark."

"How do you know?"

"I've eaten some," Juan Manuel says. "Seems a little bit like tree."

Calypso pauses for a moment. "Well, whatever the trees told them, the people were very excited."

Good Boy groans and tries to blow Thundersloth's smell out of his nose. It doesn't work. "Shriya is safe?"

"Yes, they're all fine," Juan Manuel says.

"Good. Now we can go back home."

"I think we're going soon," Calypso says.

"Unless they're excited about something more with this horrible place and want to stay here longer," says Juan Manuel.

Calypso reaches her arms out to Thundersloth, who lifts her into the tree. "Then maybe we'll just leave without them," she calls down.

In spite of the smell, Good Boy falls to sleep again and Juan Manuel lays down near him to do the same. Soon, a thunderstorm rolls in and the friends enjoy the cooling rain. Juan Manuel wishes the people could scrub Thundersloth down with some soap while it's raining, like Miguel sometimes does to himself and the other goats. Some of the goats hate it, but Juan Manuel finds it relaxing.

Shriya, Miguel, and Rondo squat inside the exit to the pyramid as giant raindrops pound the ground with a percussive roar. Streams of mud run down the fresh pile of dirt at the half-dug out entrance in random, shifting paths. Two rabbits poke their heads in, see the people, and run past them into the darkness, but Rondo doesn't notice as his eyes are focused as if he's looking at something a greater distance away than the underside of the top cover of the Spanish box that he's holding in front of them.

At first glance, they are distinct symbols, as if part of some unknown language, but with his distant focus, the blurred, shadowed symbols appear to form a single picture and a thought hits him like a bolt of lightning. He smiles, trying to contain his excitement—it's a map!

With the dark, stormy sky limiting the light, Rondo flips the top over to close the box and protect it and the book, his throbbing head floating with thoughts of how to find where the map—if it really is a map—begins, and how many of the symbols might still exist to find as reference. He laughs to himself, nothing hides from the LiDAR pictures he has of the whole area.

Shriya hears his laugh and looks at the box in his lap. "You find anything especially interesting?"

"Maybe," he offers, reluctantly. "It's going to take some research, but I might have found a clue about where the wreck of the *Santa Teresa* could be."

"Are you serious?"

"I don't think I've ever been so serious in my life."

"Is there a treasure map?" Miguel asks.

"No, there's a name of a place scribbled in a different hand at the bottom of the manifest. I think is written in blood."

"Where is it?" Miguel asks, leaning in interestedly.

"It's a small fort that I never heard of," Rondo says, "but I think I can find it. I would guess it isn't too far from here if this box and the armor . . . and the skeletons came from the fleeing survivors of the fort or the wreck like I'm thinking."

Shriya and Miguel look at each other.

"Most of those places are near cities today, aren't they?" Shriya asks. "If so, someone probably would have found the treasure by now."

"I don't think it's a city today, or I would recognize the name. There were several settlements on the coast that were heavily damaged in the storm that sunk the *Santa Teresa* and were subsequently destroyed by an unexpectedly strong force of Indigenous people after the Spanish had supposedly conquered the last major Indigenous city." Rondo stares out through the rain, seeing things no one else can see in the blur of droplets, a fuzzy and distorted picture like an old analog TV with the antennae out of adjustment. Lightning flashes and a galleon appears in the passing water, listing to port, sails either reefed or torn. Thunder cracks like a cannon and rolls like a large wooden ship smashed against the rocks at the base of the lost fort. He smiles, knowing that what he's been searching for his whole life is finally within his grasp.

Suddenly aware that Shriya is looking at him curiously, he blinks heavily and the rain washes the vision from the air. "I was just wondering if this city had been a secret. The Indigenous people could have isolated themselves here if they had known what had happened to the rest of the empire, maybe used this place to stage raids."

"Mm. So, you're not going to look for funding to come back here and be known for this discovery?" Shriya asks.

"If I'm right about this treasure, I won't be asking for funding ever again. As far as I'm concerned, the jungle can swallow this place back up, and the giant sloth is welcome to it in perpetuity."

"Good," Shriya says. "I won't have to make your death look like an accident on the way back to the boats."

"Funny. No, fame is fine, but I'm sick and tired of begging for money so I can spend it crouching in hot, dusty conditions trying to solve ancient mysteries about our shared past only to discover new ones so that the world can maybe scan a few paragraphs about it on a Reuter's daily news notification buried under endless political division." Rondo takes a long, slow breath.

"We're studying where *humanity* comes from, *our* stories, *our* rises and falls and I need to waste most of my time begging people to fund it while wealth hoarders fly private jets halfway across the world for an expensive dinner?" he says. "No, screw them. Fortune is good enough for me!"

"So you can be one of those private jet traveling diners?" Miguel almost sneers.

"God no. Those vapid, wasteful people will make up one of the reasons for our fall for future archaeologists to ponder." Rondo says. "But I would like to live a bit more comfortably, maybe live in one place year round—my own place—and it would be nice to not drive a twenty year old car that my mechanic jokingly waves his hands at me to not pull it into his lot every time I bring it to him. I got to tell you, that hand-waving joke has been quite beaten to death."

Rondo gazes down at the box again.

"The rest of the money will go to backing some projects I'd most like to support and programs to make young people more interested in history. I'll be the guy giving the grants! Having my name on the wing of a museum will be enough fame for me."

"Sounds like you've had this thought once or twice," Shriya says quietly.

"So many times that even *I'm* sick of hearing it."

"I guess I can't argue with any of that," Shriya says. "I'm in a similar situation where I'm getting tired of field work, but I don't want to work indoors and it's not like I can just jump into something different, since there's not really much else that my experience translates to."

"Would it be tough to go back to school for geology with what you already know? You could work for oil and mining companies."

"I want to be able to live with myself," she scoffs.

"Well, at least you own your own home," Rondo tells her. "Houses might be cheaper here, but they're still not cheap. Paleontology must pay better."

"The house and Zodiac are from the money my grandparents left me. My car is a Corolla, so it doesn't need the mechanic too often, but at some point, time catches up to everything. It might not be twenty years old yet, but it's not far off."

"Why don't you get in on this with me?" Rondo offers.

"I'm not chasing lost pirate treasure!"

"Where's your sense of adventure?"

"I'm leaving it here for the giant sloth to trample."

"Even if you find the treasure, you can't just go take it," Miguel says. "You're going to be tied up in courts for years as everyone and their dog makes a claim to it."

"And maybe even goats and sloths," Shriya laughs.

"What's a dog or a sloth going to do with pillaged gold?" Rondo says, shaking his head with a frown. "Look, the Spanish murdered the Indigenous people and stole it, then whatever wasn't stolen again by a French pirate was sunk in the waters of a country that didn't yet exist. So, who is the rightful thief? I'd say whoever finds it."

"It doesn't matter what you say," Miguel says, "it matters what the courts say and they allow whoever has the most power to steal whatever they want."

"Unfortunately for the courts, they can only steal what they know exists."

"Maybe it should go back to the modern day Mayans," Miguel suggests.

"Sure, and my family goes back to Mercia before William the Conqueror. Maybe I should get a share of the Saxon treasure hoards that people find."

"All I know is I've seen shows about people spending many years and millions of dollars looking for sunken treasure only to spend another decade and millions more in court fighting claims from groups who didn't spend a single colón on the search, but can somehow claim it belongs to them."

"Has anyone ever told you that you take the fun out of everything?" Rondo asks Miguel. "I'm aware of the difficulties other people have encountered, and I'm not worried."

Silence fills the cave for a moment.

"Well, boys, it looks like the rain is stopping." Shriya says. "We should probably head back to the boats. I'm starving for some real food and a long shower. I don't know which one I want more—I might end up eating *in* the shower!"

"You could have stepped outside to shower in the rain. I swear I wouldn't look," Rondo says.

"There's no soap," she says, putting her boonie hat back over her oily black hair, and climbing up the mud ramp to get outside the pyramid.

Miguel looks at Rondo and shrugs, "There's no soap."

"Nope," he says disappointedly, putting the ship's logbook back into its box. "Forget the satellite phone—*that's* what I should have brought."

Miguel sighs. "Yeah, me too."


Good Boy lifts his head at Shriya's approach, gets up, and shakes the water out of his fur. Juan Manuel sees him and does the same, shaking close to Good Boy, and getting water all over him.

"Goat!" Good Boy says with annoyance, stepping out of range to shake himself off again. Juan Manuel snorts.

Shriya reaches Good Boy and Juan Manual and bends down to them with a smile, "You boys ready to go?"

"*Bahahahaha,*" Juan Manuel says.

Good Boy barks in excitement.

The sound of barking draws Calypso awake and she stretches her head out from where she had tucked it under her arms in the sheltered crook of the tree. Good Boy is below barking and turning in an excited circle. She looks over at Thundersloth, who stares at Good Boy in annoyance before stripping another twig of its leaves with his long tongue. Shriya waves at Calypso from below and the other two people walk up to stand beside her.

They must be going back, but she's still so tired that she considers staying to avoid the long trek. She's made new friends with the rabbits and Thundersloth, even if he stinks really bad. She entertains it only a moment before Good Boy's insistent, worried barking pulls at her heart. With a long blink of resignation, Calypso begins to climb down.

By the time she reaches Juan Manuel's back, she's glad she did. The people have gathered their stuff and are waiting for her.

"Everybody ready?" Shriya asks, and Good Boy barks excitedly in a circle.

Calypso lifts a closed hand to Thundersloth, who looks confused before going back to eating.

```
        /\    /\                                    ~ \   / ~
------ \ 0 /  0 / ------|||---/o) _ (o\---|||------  (       )  ----
        \ /  \ /                                      \_/
         \/
```

As they exit through the old city entrance, Calypso's nose picks up the smell of the dead chimp from the guard tower. She looks toward the smell. "See?" she says to Good Boy and Juan Manuel, "He fell down."

The chimpanzee's resting place is obvious by the swarming flies. Good Boy looks at them for a moment before following the tree up to the platform, its open trap door creaking hauntingly in the breeze. "Did he slip?"

"Yes." Calypso says. "After I opened the door from under him."

"So, you killed him?" Juan Manuel asks.

"No, the ground did."

"So, it was a lucky mistake."

"No," Calypso says. "I meant to do it."

Good Boy looks at her in amazement.

"My mother taught that one should always have a strong grip on something stable," she explains. "He didn't."

Good Boy nods with respect. "Good work."

"If you could move fast and ate others, you really could be the most dangerous killer," Juan Manuel says. "After people, of course."

"Don't worry," Calypso assures him. "I wouldn't eat—"

*"Ar! Ar! Ar!"* rings through the air before she can finish.

They turn to see Thundersloth awkwardly galloping toward them.

*"Bahahahahahaha,"* Juan Manuel responds.

Thundersloth catches up and extends his face to the friends.

Calypso reaches to pat his nose. "You're free now! No more terrible chimpaneezees to hurt you."

He nuzzles her body with his nose some more, and she strokes the top of his face.

"This is where you should be, away from the people," she says. "You won't fit in the boat. These are my friends from a long time and I'm staying with them. Don't squash the rabbits!"

Thundersloth follows them through the rainforest until the path narrows. He turns back, and as the friends lose sight of him, all the other insects and animals in the rainforest go quiet.

*"Ahhooooooooh!"* booms from the distance.

Calypso turns around and calls back, *"Aaaahhhhiiiieeee!"*

"Good," Juan Manuel says. "I was starting to think he might try to follow us onto the boat."

"I think he was making sure we were safe," Calypso says.

"Doesn't seem like he has any friends and those chimps were terrible to him, but he liked you," Juan Manuel says.

"I like *him*. And he has friends—he has us," Calypso says. "Are you not his friends?"

"I don't know, he *did* try to kill us."

"The chimpaneezees made him do that."

"Yeah . . . he did come back and save us, so I guess I'm his friend. How about you, Good Boy?"

"He needs some baths," Good Boy sniffs.

"Yes," Calypso agrees with a tinge of impatience.

"But," Good Boy says, "he decided to help us, so he's OK."

"Seems kind of wrong to leave him all alone, then," Juan Manuel says.

"He's a sloth," Calypso says. "We don't mind being alone."

"But you're coming back with us," Juan Manuel says. "You could just as easily stay here. You'd even have him and the rabbits for company if you wanted."

"Some friends are only your friends for a short time," Calypso says. "It doesn't mean you stop liking them or caring about them, just that the branch they're climbing and the branch you're climbing split off in different directions. Or *path*, if you prefer that to branches."

"That makes sense, I guess," Juan Manuel agrees. "For an animal that mostly hangs around munching leaves in slow motion, you sure know a lot."

"I don't know if I know a lot, but all that slow living leaves a lot of time to think."

## Six is a Crowd

The boats are both present and intact, if more than a little filthy for their days left alone in a rainforest filled with curious critters. Dirty footprints and scat from all manner of birds, small mammals, and reptiles cover their water-spotted decks.

Shriya pulls the drain plug on her Zodiac, and as the filthy water pours out onto her wrist, she curses herself for forgetting to remove it before leaving it on the river bank. She wipes her wrist on her torn, worn, and dirt-caked pants and lifts the bow of the boat a little to get as much water out as possible.

"Who's taking the Zodiac?" she asks, lowering the boat back down and bending by the stern to screw the plug back in.

"I'll take it," Rondo says.

"You want Miguel to go with you?"

"No, I'm fine by myself."

"Trying to get rid of me?" Miguel asks Shriya from the back of the Speedwell where he is reconnecting the ignition.

"No," she says. "He's injured and I thought he might need a hand plus it's going to get crowded and really smelly with all the animals on the Speedwell."

"At this point, it's me who should apologize to them for the smell," Miguel winces.

Juan Manuel and Good Boy turn to each other and nod in agreement.

"What did he say?" Calypso asks.

"He said he stinks."

"Oh. Yes, he does. You all do, but I don't complain."

"You complain all the time!" Juan Manuel says.

"Hm. Yes, but not as much as I think about it."

"I can take Calypso," Rondo offers.

Juan Manuel, with Calypso on his back, takes a few steps away from him. Good Boy curls his lips, just slightly.

Shriya smiles at Juan Manuel and points at the Zodiac. "Calypso can drive the Speedwell if we need her to. You want to take Charleston?"

*"Bahahahahahaha!"* Juan Manuel protests, finishing with a raspberry.

"I guess not!" Shriya laughs.

"It's OK. I told you, I'm fine by myself," Rondo says. "I've got my treasure chest to keep me company. Like Louis LeFleur, but this boat doesn't need a crew. I'll follow you back, though I won't mind if you keep an eye on me just in case."

He points to the door in the front of the center console of the boat. "Do you have a key for this locker?"

"It's open," Shriya says.

"Good. It will be nice to be able to set this thing down. For a fairly small box, it weighs a ton. I swear someone has been adding lead to it every mile!"

"You really think that will guide you to the shipwreck?"

"I think it should point me in the general direction."

"There should be a bottle of ibuprofen in there, too. It's been sitting in some heat, but it might be worth a shot."

"Got it! Bottled water, too? You're a life saver. You need some water? There's a full case of a dozen in here."

"Perfect!" Shriya exclaims. "I forgot that was there. We can take two thirds. I'm sure the animals could use some, too."

"Works for me," Rondo says, taking out four bottles for himself and handing her the rest.

With the boats loaded and the animals laying in the back of the Speedwell, they all head down the river with the people trying to ignore the itching of a thousand bug bites.

"Calypso is already asleep, just like the sloth reputation would suggest," Miguel says, leaning behind and patting her head gently as she lays on Juan Manuel. "Who would even think she could do the things we've seen her do? If they weren't so slow, it's the descendants of sloths that might rule the world today instead of the descendants of monkeys."

"Sloths have a very slow metabolism," Shriya says. "Well, at least tree sloths do. They don't get much energy from their food, so their bodies adapted to not need much. Knowing that makes what she does even more incredible. Think of how tired we are and now imagine how she must feel with less than a tenth of the calories we're supposed to have!"

"You could maybe expect aggressive animals that live in groups, like dogs and goats, to risk themselves for their friends, but sloths are passive loners," Miguel says, turning away from the sleeping animals. "What could drive Calypso to be so brave?"

"Love," Shriya says with a hint of disappointment.

Miguel smiles. "Yeah. Love."

Leaning against the seat in back, Juan Manuel falls asleep to the drone of the engine, the rhythmic sloughing of the water under the hull, the comfort of his friends, his fatigued muscles, and just a little bit of well-earned soreness in his neck that doesn't so much hurt as make him proud to have been able to fight for everyone and get them all safely out of danger.

Good Boy lies near him, a little hot and a lot tired and even more hungry, but relieved that they're safe and heading home. He thinks again of Pablo and their times going out on the boat with Calypso to get food. He will always miss Pablo, but he's grateful for the friends he has today and his part in saving them. It feels like his war is over and he can rest.

Calypso is asleep on Juan Manuel looking drained, but otherwise unfazed by the adventure. Maybe sloths have it all figured out, Good Boy thinks as the boat reaches the open water. Shriya slides the canopy back for air and opens up the throttle. From behind, Good Boy hears Rondo doing the same. The cool ocean air tumbles into the boat and whirls around in the back to pull out the heat, gently rustling his fur. Soon he's comfortably asleep.

Warm and relaxed by the rise and fall of Juan Manuel breathing beneath her, a thoroughly exhausted Calypso sleeps. She dreams not of trees and leaves, but of where she is right now. Well, there are *some* leaves, but almost any leaves will do as long as she's with her friends.

Stephen Kappotis grew up on the North Shore of Massachusetts and enjoys writing, design, history, zoology, wood working, machines, and making things.

The idea for this series began while working on a compact speedboat design that uses an aircraft-inspired control stick for steering and motor trim while watching videos of rescued sloths opening doors, using a toilet (more or less), and teaching these skills to others. At one point, the image of a sloth operating the boat's simple controls came to him and he began to wonder what her story could be. Being a sloth, she needed a faster way to get around on land, which led to a dog character for her to ride like a horse. Not wanting to simply write anthropomorphized animal characters, he attempted to account for the differences in perspective that would come from the varying lifestyles and senses of the characters while balancing an ability to communicate in a manner needed for the story. Inspired by old myths of capricious gods and flawed heroes overcoming their often humble origins to accomplish great feats and triumph over powerful adversaries, the story soon developed into this series. *The Voyages of Sloth and Good Boy.*